A STRETCH
on the RIVER

A STRETCH on the RIVER

RICHARD BISSELL

with an afterword by
Martha C. Bray

Minnesota Historical Society • St. Paul • 1987

Borealis Books are high-quality paperback reprints of books chosen by the Minnesota Historical Society Press for their importance as enduring historical sources and their value as enjoyable accounts of life in the Upper Midwest.

MINNESOTA HISTORICAL SOCIETY PRESS, ST. PAUL 55101

International Standard Book Number 0-87351-220-0

Manufactured in the United States of America

10   9   8   7   6   5   4   3   2   1

Library of Congress Cataloging-in-Publication Data
Bissell, Richard Pike.
   A stretch on the river.

Reprint. Originally published: Boston : Little,
Brown, 1950.
   I. Title.
PS3552.I772914S7   1987   813'.54   87-20390
ISBN 0-87351-220-0 (alk. paper)

To R. C.

The years which Mr. Clemens had passed on the Mississippi, and the rough life of California, lacked greatly the refining influence of a different civilization.

With that sharp schooling he had become too well acquainted with all the coarser types of human nature.

— MRS. THOMAS BAILEY ALDRICH

1

SOMETIMES in the early summer evenings in those days you could hear the steam calliope playing on the hurricane deck of the steamer *Capitol* to drum up trade for the moonlight excursion. They would play "Beautiful Ohio" and "I'm Forever Blowing Bubbles," and after a rest period, during which the calliope player would stroll to and fro on the deck smoking a good cigar, perhaps we would hear "Dardanella." My brother Herb and I used to go down and sit on the railroad tracks by the levee and watch the black deckhands wheeling coal aboard, and smell the damp smell of steam and steam cylinder oil that floated out of the engine room. Herb would rather be the pilot but I would rather be the calliope player or the deckhand that handled the lines on the big red capstan at every landing.

By now the calliope player and the *Capitol* are dead, and Herb no longer would be satisfied with a pilot's job. I'm the simple one in the family. I'd still like to throw the lines on that big red capstan, and I'd still like to play that steam piano for a moonlight excursion to Winona or Red Wing, and hear the music come back to me from the Sugar Loaf or Barn Bluff.

Then in the winter I used to take the streetcar down the hill on Saturday afternoon, and sit there in the third row at the Rialto, getting sick on peanut butter kisses, all choked up from the violin music, and see myself in future years as an all-American hero such as racing driver with cap on backwards, fireman carrying beautiful girl in nightie down the high ladder, lounge lizard in dress suit, or leather pusher with several coeds in coat-style shaker-knit sweaters cheering from the ringside. I was going to do big things in those days — all I needed was the clothes for the different parts. Pass the peanut brittle.

The psychiatrists, phrenologists, and my sister-in-law would say that the way things worked out for me was all because of a blurred parent pattern or a secondary marginal

Oedipus rejection. (I am glad I didn't have to pay a bill for that revelation.)

Papa was the society bootlegger when I was a kid and then after repeal he made a pile with his two aristocratic old-time saloons. Oh, he wasn't a little fat guy in an outsize overcoat passing bottles of gin in paper bags through the back door — he sold only good stuff, by the case, to the boys at the Elks Club, and gave humorous speeches at Rotary in a double-breasted gray flannel.

"I'm Bill Joyce, and this here is my brother Herb," I used to say.

"Dan Joyce your daddy?"

"Yes, sir."

"Well, well, I'm a pretty good friend of your daddy's. I don't suppose you and your brother would like an ice cream soda?"

That's the way it used to go. That's the way it was all the time.

All we would have needed in town to be a big hit was the money. But on top of all the money he made, Papa was a personality, an institution.

I got through school in the usual ludicrous manner: wore a bedsheet toga in the Latin Club play, drove a splinter right through my hand when we knocked down the Cedar Rapids goalposts, and had many a nice afternoon with Jane Schofield and her sister Helen and Fritz Hindenberg up in the loft of the Schofield carriage house. This was back in the days when the old carriage houses still smelled of horses instead of crankcase oil, even though the horses had long since gone to the glue works, the days before they commenced calling girls Karen and Darlene and Linda Mae, and also the days when some of the girls, if not all, wore bloomers.

I was pretty fresh in high school. I was only about 138 pounds, wore my hair slicked down and parted in the middle and a snake ring on my right hand, not to mention a big shaggy fur coat that Papa got me from one of his eggish friends out on Roosevelt Road in Chicago, and just at the time when Harold Teen and all the simps were wearing them. But except for Jack Schwartz I was the only one in high school that had a fur coat, and his was just his brother's coonskin, not his at all. The coonskin created quite a stir and made me pretty sick, but after thinking it over the girls decided I was cute after all; besides, all Jack could think of to boost his popularity was to buy extra-thick malteds for everybody and flash five-dollar bills, and once in a while borrow his brother's Marmon phaeton. Most of the jazz-mad members of the rampant age wanted roadsters but Jack's brother Jefferson got a phaeton because he could get two or three cases back there and passengers too; he also had some other more conventional ideas about the back seat. Jack did get a good deal of credit when he could borrow the Marmon, but after a while nobody would ride with him as his idea was to emulate Wally Reid as much as possible, and the way he took corners, why once was plenty for the customers in the back seat.

Pretty soon I got so hard to bear that Papa took me over to Chicago to Maurice Rothschild's and bought me some clothes and a wardrobe trunk as big as a Locomobile and sent me off to a school between four and five thousand years old down in New Hampshire, although I wanted to stay home and play the comic part in *Margie's Chance,* the senior class play.

I was there just long enough to figure out the accents before being bounced out and then I was home again and all I had learned was how to check my trunk on a through ticket. There were a lot of queer ones down in New England, but nobody seemed to notice; however, there are some nuts right out here in the Golden West that are blue ribbon contenders and you don't have to hire a radio cab and go outside the city limits to find them.

So I went to a military school with nineteen students and a howitzer on the lawn and learned a good deal from a boy from Indianapolis but nothing much about how to wage war or handle the *épée.* My brother Herb wanted to go to college so he went to old man Thorwald, the principal of high school, for some advice. Thorwald, who was a graduate soil chemist from South Dakota State (and therefore an ideal high school principal), told Herb that St. Olaf was the best college in the country but Herb told him he wasn't a Lutheran and if he was he wouldn't want to be a preacher. So Herb went to the U. of Illinois and took a course covering Proust's asthma. Presently he astonished everyone by marrying a sensational queen from Cincinnati whose family owned a string of hotels and nine brick factories with tall chimneys. And no kids except Herb's wife. They got married accompanied by a large shipment of champagne and some girls in marquisette dresses, and father-in-law bought Herb the Palace Hotel back home for a wedding present. My brother is a bird, all right.

Meanwhile, I was sampling the nation's educational institutions. Finally a bunch of us took our roadsters down to a college in Confederate territory, and after that one I was finished. If Honest Abe had met some of the jelly beans I went to school with down there he would have called off the war and spent the money on a wall instead.

Papa was running his two good money-making places now, the Trocadero and the Five Mile House, both across the river in Illinois. We had a big house up on Westview Avenue, and a yard with hard maple trees, and Papa joined the Country Club. Once upon a time the Country Club was quite an exclusive group of fish, but later all you had to do to get in was be willing to kiss the old girls who got liquored up, and be able to throw up at dances without getting it on your shoes.

Everything was going fine at home and Papa was making a lot of money and Herb was all set, so I went to Europe to conclude my investigations.

Two years later it had become 1937 and I had a headache.

I bought mosaic brooches for all the girls and started for home. In the afternoons I was sad, and on the return trip I sat in the men's bar of an antique Cunarder playing "I've Found a New Baby" and "Monday Date" on the upright piano, while the spray of the North Atlantic in November settled on the windows of the promenade deck.

Then I came home one night, and Papa was there at the depot in a chesterfield and bowler hat, and Herb and

Sis, with the Duesenberg, and the cold Midwestern rain pattered on the ancient brick streets.

So far my life had been lacking in direction and I was well aware of the hopelessness of everything. For the next few years I played the game and hit the line hard for the furniture factory, Herb's newest enterprise, and offended untold numbers of citizens with my polo coat with the six-inch lapels. Sometimes I would go down and sit by the Mississippi and watch the strong current from Minnesota sliding under the bridge bound for Basin Street, and once more I would plan great things for myself, and go home and play the piano all night. Who shall know the anguish of a proud young man?

Then, when all America had reached the ultimate in boredom, came resurrection for all the lost young men who weren't having any fun: the war. In order to maintain my standing with the girls, and in joyous anticipation of an honorable exit, I went to Chicago to secure a handsome navy uniform.

They told me to take off my glasses and read the chart. That was all that was necessary and I was back on La Salle Street again in ten minutes, like a character from *Bound to Rise* about to hunt up a cheap but clean eating establishment.

"They told me I got bum eyes," I said, when I had got home and made myself comfortable at the end of the bar at the Sixty-Six, Papa's new place. It had a walnut bar out of the old Congress Hotel in Chicago, and the only beer sold was National Premium in bottles, from Baltimore. Papa knew how to drag in the boys with money.

[9]

"Tough luck, kid," said Jack Schwartz from behind a necktie with a skyrocket on it.

"What the hell do I need eyes in the navy for?"

"Well, maybe the army will take you. Did you try them yet?" Jack said, and ordered up some more of the Catto's twelve-year-old.

"Gimme another, Marc," I said. It was about 4 P.M., a bad hour. "And a little more ice." Marc had been with Papa since the old days when we had the Chicago connection.

My thoughts about the army will remain unprinted.

A small but useful girl named Adele squeezed my hand. She smelled delicious, a blend of fur and teatime kisses. Marc leaned against the back bar and treated himself to a small Hennessy.

A few weeks later the ice in the river broke up and went south, and the first steamboats bound for St. Paul came up past town and blew for the drawbridge. The kids flew kites on the aphrodisiac spring breezes. Life at the factory was a history of futility, arguing with the salesmen and checking delinquent accounts. Adele, Bunny, Francine, Tootie all did their best, but everything seemed unreal in 1942 — a dream that would have no ending.

Meanwhile the boys were going, going, going. Jack Schwartz took a course in welding, removed the double-breasted sharkskin and was last seen heading in the general direction of a shipyard at Seneca, Illinois. Whether he got there I can't say for sure, but at least he didn't resume occupancy of bar stool number three at the Sixty-Six until all the boys had quit discharging firearms at each other. Another enthusiast for the army.

Then, on an unimportant day when the gods had decreed that nothing was ever to happen to me again beyond success as a party piano player, the flood waters of fate broke the dam, and I found myself at last floundering in the torrent. It was a desperate afternoon and everyone in the world seemed to be living but me. I left Myrtle to stall on the incoming calls and went over to the Sixty-Six to rest up for the evening. There was nobody in the bar but the radio and Georgie Whiting, an old boy from high school, now one of our local steamboat pilots. I bought Georgie a couple of Old Hickorys and in no time he was telling me what a sweet deal he had on the river — how much money he made, how many girls there were in St. Louis, and how the draft board never bothered him, or any of the boys on the boats.

"Look at them haw trees in bloom all over the hills," he said. "Bill, steamboating on the Upper Mississippi is like the old days in high school when you woke up and jumped out of bed in the morning and looked out the window just to see if the wonderful world was out there waiting for you." This Georgie was quite a poet, a shot-put champ, and president of the Biology Club. "That world is still outside, Bill, but you never see it if you hang around this dump and spend your time with Schwartz and the rest of them mutts."

"I'm a city kid, Georgie," I said.

Then he told me how his company was looking for

bright young fellows to be pilots, captains, general traffic managers, personnel directors, and candidates for the U. S. Senate. The company was young, he said, and growing fast. They were pushing the younger men and looking for a high type personnel.

"Well, Georgie," I said, "I'm strictly a high type personnel, but is there any glory in it?"

"Glory! Why Bill, you can *live* on the boats."

"I better get in the army, Georgie. They're already starting to talk."

"I love that line," Georgie said. "All our lives we been reading Remarque and telling each other what a line of cheese all that war stuff is. Now the Community Band goes down the street with the cornets playing flat on the high notes and right away you wanna get in the army. Smarten up, Bill. You and I don't have to prove nothing. The one thing we got in common is we don't give a damn for nobody or nothing."

People were doing the most peculiar things in those days.

"Smarten up, boy," he said. "Leave the dumbbells settle the war. Remember the line we was brought up on? 'Cannon fodder.' Remember Paul Baumer? Remember Katczinsky? Smarten up."

"Wouldn't it be pretty obvious if all of a sudden a big capitalist like me decided to go off decking on an old Upper Mississippi towboat?" I said.

"Obvious to who? It'd be obvious to me that you was a man. By God you'll know you're alive once you get aboard."

Two more of Marc's highballs and I had made up my mind.

Papa was amazed.

"Who's the president of this outfit? Maybe I can fix you up," he said. "What's your angle, boy?"

"Never mind, Papa," I said. "I'm going out and look at the sky for a while and see if I can figure things out."

"So long, kid," Herb said. "I don't know what this is all about, but you must have a slant on it."

"I'm going for a boat ride," I said. "I'll probably be home in a week."

And then I was in St. Louis in the Union Station, and then I was in a Checker cab, and then I was aboard the Diesel towboat *Inland Coal,* and the lights of St. Louis sparkled in the sky, and the cars crossed Eads Bridge, and they gave me a bunk and a blanket.

"What do they call you?" the Second Mate said.

"Call me Ishmael," I said.

That ain't no real swearin what that mate
done. I can do's good's that m'self.

— CHARLES EDWARD RUSSELL

2

WE were out on the foredeck.

"What's the matter, stud, didn't you never see the sunrise before?" the Second Mate said to me.

"Not since I can remember it," I said, looking at the pink clouds over the Illinois hills.

"Well, you're not likely to miss a single one from now on," he said. "Pretty, ain't it?"

The other two deckhands on the watch came out on deck pulling on their gloves.

"Shorty, you and Diamond go on out and clean up the rigging on the head of 112," the Second Mate said. And to me he said, "Come here, stud, I wanna talk to you."

He sat down on a timberhead and watched the sunrise. He was about thirty-five years old and his face and his Grecian nose were tanned from twenty years of river weather. I liked his blond hair sticking out from under the blue Mate's cap, and better still his mouth, which seemed much more inclined to smile than to sneer. Evidently things had not yet begun to get him down. He was about six feet of Mate, with shoulders to match, and I wondered how many girls he had on the Upper Mississippi.

The deckhands went out on the barges.

"They're sending us some strange ones these days under the name of deckhands," he said, "but up to now we ain't had no college boys. What the hell's the matter with you, stud? This job is too rough even for a farm boy."

"What gives you this college boy idea?" I said.

"Why, kid, it was sticking out all over you when you come aboard."

"I suppose it was. How was it?"

"First you had on a hand-tied bow tie instead of the jazzbow model. Next your short haircut. Last, when I showed you where your bunk was at in the pigpen you says 'Thanks.' Now nobody but a college boy would be enough of a fool to say 'Thanks' for an introduction to a dirty bunk. You college boys are all the time saying 'Thanks,' 'Thanks a lot,' 'Thanks old boy,' and all that crap. If you would of growled a little bit or maybe cussed the company when you seen your luxurious sleeping accommodations, I wouldn't of been so sure, in spite of the bow tie."

I began to laugh. This bird was pretty funny.

"Well," I said, "I can let my hair grow out easy enough, throw away the bow tie, and eliminate the 'Thanks old boy.' "

"Yeah," he said. "You ought to do that. That is, if you was going to stay. But you ain't, stud, you won't be on here long enough to tell the bow from the stern."

"Oh yes I will," I said. "I'll be around for a while. Anyway long enough for my hair to grow out."

"No you won't, kid," he said. "I hate to tell you, but the truth is, you'll never even see St. Paul. This here is the craziest life on earth, and for a guy who ain't use to misery a deckhand's life is unnecessary torture. You'll soon see there ain't no sense to it."

"I'll be here when we get to St. Paul," I said.

"No you won't. You'll be all disgusted before we get to Rock Island. By the time we get to Lynxville you'll get off, if you can crawl by that time."

"Listen, Mister," I said, "how about me going out and getting to work with the rest of the watch? If it's so damn rough I'll get off, if I like it I'll stay."

"Well, you ain't gonna like it. And on the river you don't need to call me Mister. My name is Joe."

"You're the Mate," I said. "I better not call you Joe."

"Listen stud, relax. This ain't the *Queen Mary*, just an old Upper Mississippi towboat that needs an engine overhaul. Everybody from Minneapolis to Cairo calls me Joe, so don't feel that it's a big treat."

"All right," I said.

"Your problem is gonna be keeping up with the work and trying to get enough sleep to keep alive. If you can hold out for a month without getting discouraged you might make it, if you're stubborn. But I don't see why you even care to try."

"They got a draft board in my home town just like everyplace else," I said.

"Now we're getting someplace. You ain't ascared to go and fight, are you?"

"No. I just don't like the god damn army. I guess I read too many books about the other war. It don't appeal to me."

"They pulled all my brother's teeth, the bastards. Never had a toothache in his life."

"The navy turned me down. 'All right then,' I said, 'the hell with you and the hell with the whole damn thing. I'll go and work on a tugboat then if you don't want me.' "

" 'How come they pulled your teeth?' I says to my brother. 'How do I know?' he says. 'Go and ask the U. S. Army,' he says, 'they don't know neither. And they don't welcome questions.' "

"Was he sick?"

"You ought to follow him pitching hay if you think he was sick. He was about as sick as Charles Atlas."

"Well, there you have a perfect example," I said.

"Leave me give you one little nickel's worth of bum advice, kid," he said. "I been out here on the river a long time."

[18]

"What's that?"

"If you're really set on staying here, keep pretty quiet for a while until the other deckhands get used to you. Do your work and keep your mouth shut. If they see you can hold up your end making tow in a rainstorm they'll soon forget about the college stuff. Don't try and big talk the other deckhands. Pretty soon you'll find them giving you a few pointers on the work. Watch what they do. Watch how they pick up a ratchet and set it on their shoulder. This Shorty on your watch is one of the best deckhands on the Upper River. Just study him and do like he does and someday you'll be a deckhand." He lit a cigarette and threw the match in the river. "Then you can write the president of that college and tell him the big news."

"All right," I said. "I'll do what I can."

"You can't do no more than that," Joe said. "There's one thing you can do for me, though."

"What's that?"

"Show me how to tie one of them god damn bow ties."

The morning wore along and I followed the other two deckhands around. I found out I didn't know anything worth knowing. I couldn't see any sense in most of the things they were doing but I didn't let on.

Then there was the matter of carrying ratchets.

"Go ahead, let me see you pick it up," I said to this sawed-off deckhand they called Shorty.

"Well, you just grab her by this here link and up-end her, get your shoulder down a little, toss her on your shoulder and raise up." Shorty went through all this with beautiful precision and ended up with the ratchet over his shoulder.

"You make that look easy," I said.

"Aw listen, don't you worry none, I couldn't do it neither when I first come onto a steamboat," he said. "I use to pick 'em up by main strength and awkwardness and carry 'em in my arms instead of on the shoulder. Another thing, if you close your links before you pick it up, they won't be abangin your back and aclonkin your knees whilst you walk out on the barges."

Shorty's homely face and crooked grin made you want to laugh. With his shaggy hair and awkward gait he had *farmer* written all over him. And although he'd been on the river for years he still wore his farm clothes — blue bib overalls, blue chambray shirt, blue denim harvest jacket, and hickory-stripe shop cap. He wasn't so short, but he was stocky, and the name seemed to fit. And he was a real person, nobody ever laughed at him. That grin of his helped out on the dark days.

The other deckhand was leaning against the main capstan. He wasn't giving out any information.

"Now leave me see you pick it up," Shorty said.

I'd been sitting around the bar at the Sixty-Six so long about all the muscles I had left were the ones in my fingers from holding onto a glass. Well, I got the ratchet up on my shoulder but I was about through for the day and ready for a rubdown from the effort. A ratchet is a double-end screw jack weighing about the same as Stanislaus Zbyszko.

"I guess you ain't been workin very hard lately," Shorty said.

The other deckhand looked like he agreed with this analysis. He said nothing, however.

"Now, when you throw her down, get out of the way as she's droppin so you don't get a link on your foot. Duke Robinette off the *James W. Good* is up at the St. Louie marine hospital right this minute from droppin a ratchet on his foot. I seen the Mate down at Wood River last night and he told me. 'How did it happen, Blackie?' I says. 'Why the dumb Peoria bastard dropped a ratchet on his foot, that's how it happened,' he says. 'I never dropped one on my foot yet,' I says. 'Turtle Peterson over on the *Locke Tarleton*, he dropped one on his foot when we was up Cumberland River, two years ago Thanksgiving,' he says. 'I ain't seen Turtle since we was on the *Black Diamond* together,' I says. 'He never dropped no ratchets on the *Black Diamond*,' I says, 'because he never had aholt of one. He was layin asleep in the deck room most of the time.'"

"The *Black Diamond* burned up down on the Ohio," the other deckhand said.

"Now listen," Shorty said, "don't I know the *Black Diamond* burned up down on the Ohio? Don't I know it was right below Caseyville? Don't I know Cat Brown burned up on her? Don't I know it was on a Christmas Eve and the engineer was drunk? Don't I . . ."

"All right. All *right*," said the other deckhand.

"Listen," I said, "I gotta learn how to splice. They'll probably fire me if I don't learn to splice."

[21]

"Have you got leprosy or third degree cholery?"

"Not that I know of," I said.

"Well then, don't worry about gettin fired," Shorty said. "Deckhands are so scarce they're thinkin of importing 'em from Arkansaw."

"Why Arkansaw?" I said.

"Well, they claim they didn't hear about the war yet down there and they say there is plenty of strong boys in the back country that would make deckhands."

"Did you ever hear that radio station they got down at Blytheville?" the other deckhand said.

"No, I never heard it," Shorty said.

"They just play and sing and yodel all the time. They don't have nothing else on the programs. Mostly yodeling and blues."

"My old man used to know Jimmy Rodgers," I said. Right away I remembered what Joe had told me and I knew I should never have said that.

The other deckhand decided the time had come to notice that I was here.

"You say your old man knew Jimmy Rodgers?"

"Yeah," I said. "He met him once down in Memphis."

"Can your old man sing blues and yodel?"

"No," I said. "My old man's in the whiskey and hootch business."

"Whiskey and hootch? My lands," Shorty said.

"Now what do you call those cables there?" I said.

"Them's the face wires. Never mind them. Do you get whiskey free when you're at home?" the other deckhand said.

"Why sure," I said. "And what do you call these cables here?"

"Them's the jockey wires," the other deckhand said. "My oh my, imagine an old man in the whiskey business."

"Don't he sell no wine?" Shorty said.

"Sure," I said. "Anything you want. Why do you call them the jockey wires?"

"I'm more partial to wine," Shorty said. "Elderberry wine to my mind is about as good a drink as you'll find."

"How come they call these here the jockey wires?" I said.

"Why man, because that's their *name*, that's why," Shorty said. "Elderberry wine is mostly homemade, though. I don't suppose your old man handles it."

Well, there I was. Joe had told me not an hour before to keep my mouth shut but of course I had to blow off about Papa and Jimmy Rodgers. It was not having any bad results, though. They both seemed to think I was a little less useless right away.

"Another thing," I said. "What's this 'jackknifing' I hear you talking about?"

"Why that's when we bust up the barges and nest them up to lock through. You'll see it soon enough, right up at Saverton Lock."

"I think I better learn to splice. We seem to bust a lot of ropes."

"Lines, man, *lines*. We ain't got no ropes aboard," Shorty said.

"Well, we ain't doing nothing much," the other deck-

hand said. "Come on down in the hole, you, and I'll show
you an eye splice."

I figured I was getting along all right.

It was a long trip to St. Paul all the same. I was pretty
well worn out and had a smashed-up foot and a couple
of mashed fingers. But I thought I would be all right after
I could learn to sleep. We worked six hours on and six hours
off, week after week. By the time you made the sack and
got to sleep you had lost nearly an hour. To eat and make
watch time you lost half an hour. That meant that the
most sleep you could ever get at one time was four and a
half or five hours, but I couldn't get this much.

The deckhands' bunkroom ran athwartships right aft of
the engine room. As you lay in your sway-backed bunk
plucking the shoddy 12 per cent wool blanket, only a three-
sixteenths-inch steel bulkhead separated your head from
two 800-horsepower Diesel engines. Every so often the
whole boat would go into a violent shudder. If through
exhaustion I fell asleep in spite of the noise and the vibra-
tion, then we would arrive at a lock and the engines would
stop, and I would awake from the unusual silence. Then
I would toss and listen to the popping of the compressed air
as we maneuvered for an hour locking through.

Joe took me uptown in St. Paul while we were waiting
for empties. His girl was Irene and she got me a girl and
we went out. My girl's name was Merle. I was surprised
she was so good looking. But I was so beat up I didn't realize
she was actually beautiful until I got to thinking about it
later.

"How about a drink?" I said.

"I don't mind," she said.

"Whiskey?" I said.

"Whiskey and sour."

"Want to dance?"

"I s'pose so."

"This your home town?"

"Uh uh."

"Where do you come from?"

"Eveleth."

"That's up in the iron range."

"Uh huh."

"What your folks do up there?"

"My dad's in the mine."

"How come you came to St. Paul?"

"Didn't like it in the sticks."

"Honey, I don't blame you. I hate the sticks too."

"Where d'you get that 'honey' stuff?"

"Want a cigarette?"

"I don't mind."

Well, that went on until around midnight when we took the girls home. We all did a little high school style loving and then Joe and I went back to the boat much refreshed.

That was my first trip to St. Paul on the *Inland Coal* with Joe. I was on her a long time after that.

If you can read this, you are too darn close.

3

A LONG TIME went by, even a year.

At first I stayed out of stubbornness. Then I began to forget I had ever lived any other way. Then I began to feel sorry for the people on the bank. When I got that far I was a river man.

And there was the girl from the iron range. And there was Joe.

[27]

One afternoon we were ashore down in Alton, twenty miles north of St. Louis. Out in the street it was 96° and still going up.

"Strictly eatin stuff," said Joe.

"Yum yum," I replied and we threw down our doubles of some rare old booze that had been aged in a football bladder for about two weeks.

"Look at them boosoms," Joe said, ordering up another pair of doubles. When you get off the steamboat you have to drink fast to make up for lost time.

The subject of our remarks, a black-haired number who had just entered the air conditioning, sat down at the bar and made the usual demand, a whiskey *and* sour. Someday, if I live that long, maybe I'll meet a girl out here who doesn't want a whiskey *and* sour.

Joe, who was the Second Mate, was all decked out, and even my brother Herb would have OK'd the gabardine suit. His stylish cravat was a hair raiser, on the other hand.

We closed in on the brunette.

"You guys work on the boats?" the bartender said to me; he was a floater if I ever saw one.

"Yeh. We're waiting on our loads. Just got in from St. Paul an hour ago and the way it looks up at the tipple we'll be heading right back up the river before dark." I began to think about St. Paul, and Joe started to turn on the steam with the brunette.

St. Paul was so far away. So far away in the northland, with the trains coming in from Winnipeg, the great big electric figure 1 on top of the bank building that you can see pretty near to Duluth, the pale yellow streetcars crossing the bridges, and my baby swinging her little ass along past the Emporium while all the boys turned to look at her. Remember Merle, the beautiful girl from Eveleth? Well, she was now the big heart throb with me. After that first date she quit saying "uh uh" to everything and a red-hot love affair developed that colored the sunsets as far west as Spokane.

"How you like that there steamboatin?" said the bartender.

An interesting question.

"I like it fine," I said.

And between me and my girl the full length of the Upper Mississippi now extended: six hundred and forty long miles of twisting bends, sand bars and crossings, channel lights, day marks, swing bridges, lift bridges, floating bridges, wing dams, landings, locks, rock riprap, willows silent in the summer heat, bluffs, ancient sloughs where the kingfishers squeak, shores, towheads, cutoffs, islands, cottonwoods, catfish, clouds, and all the beautiful birch- and cedar-covered hillsides, and the river towns where the little girls stand in their pinafores on the limestone slab sidewalks watching the towboats go by.

This joint we were in had a sign, LONGEST BAR IN WESTERN ILLINOIS, which was supposed to compensate for the type of beverages they were handing around to the customers. They also got a nickel more for the highballs on account of this added feature, bringing the total to thirty-five cents. Out in the street kids were being dragged along by the hand, and the smell of melting tar and squashed Mormon flies filled the air. Down at the corner pool hall overlooking the river-front park where the interurban trains took off for St. Louis, the boys were slumped in the observers' chairs beside the rich greensward of the tables reading *Super Comics* and *Sex Detective*.

"Say, um, buddy, what do they pay for cook on them there boats?" the bartender asked, and here we go, boys, here's another one wants to go — by god they all want to go steamboating.

"I always had it in the back of my mind I'd like one a them boat jobs. Is them jobs hard to get?" and he turned to slant a high-ball glass under the spigot marked GRIESE- DIECK. He put a couple inches in the glass and drank it slowly, dreaming of a soft job on a nice sternwheel steamboat, with red, white and blue lights, a ten-cent straight cigar, and the band playing selections from *The Bohemian Girl.*

"Where did you say he was at now, Camp Edwards?" said Joe to the brunette. If that was her husband it was a nice convenient distance to have him away. She was elbowed on the bar, letting the whiskey rise in her temples, and she smoked a cigarette. Brown eyes, kissproof lips and a diamond ring.

"Gimme another," I said, and slid my glass through the puddles on the bar. "They pay about a hundred and forty."

What is there to do in these small towns except get in some tavern and sit, sit, sit, wear out a bar stool, think about all the places you could be if you weren't here, how if you don't hurry you'll never see Madagascar. Then you feel restless and you go out and wander around town and look in the window of the printing shop, lean against a telephone pole for a while, make the circuit of the dime store and sit on a park bench for a while. Get in another tavern with the same Korn Kurls, peanuts, and punch boards. All the time you are on the boat you think of the brilliant things you would do if you were only over on the bank; then you get ashore and go and sit and read the beer signs over the bar and talk to some bartender with an IQ of 20 degrees Fahrenheit.

Well, Joe was giving Miss Alton quite a going over.

"No, honest to god, I *like* that way you got your hair fixed up. Kinda like Norma Shearer, ain't it?"

"Woo, woo," says the girl.

"Hey Joe, come here a minute," I said and made the trip back to the can, past the tables with the beer mats stuck to them.

"I can see you got a grizz for this," I said. "But remember we got to get back to the boat in time to make up and take off up the river. Take it easy, huh? She won't give you any without a campaign anyway."

"You're a cheerful bastard, ain't you?" says Joe. "What do you think about on all them lonesome nights on the barge line?"

"I think about St. Paul," I said.

"Well start thinking about Alton, cause that's where **we** are. Tomorrow you might be dead."

"Anyway," I said, "Merle wouldn't like me to go out with some wild woman here in Alton."

"What! Why boy — didn't you tell me she goes out with some auto mechanic or other?"

"She don't do nothing with him."

"Wise up, Bill — we'll all be dead before we know it. Listen, this girl has her own apartment."

"That sounds a little better." Anyplace would be better than these taverns; they were all dumps and smelled of stale beer. Papa wouldn't take ten of them for a gift.

"Maybe she's got a girl friend," I said.

"Now you're in there, boy," said Joe, using a pink pocket comb.

"In where?" I said. "If I miss the boat and get canned I'll be in a scratchy brown suit within twenty minutes, with somebody outside my acquaintance shooting at me or vice versa. That draft board would just love to give me a ticket."

"Sargent ain't going to can you. He ain't going to can me. He ain't going to can nobody that knows a steel barge from a streetcar. Anyway, I thought you got turned down by the navy on account of the glasses."

"That's the navy. The draft board in my home town is taking anybody into the army who can tell night from day."

We went back to the bar and commenced all over.

"I use to cook for the CCC's and I'd sure like that there steamboat job," said the bartender to me.

"Say honey," Joe said, "less get out of here pretty soon and go over to your place."

"There ain't too much work to that job, would you say?" the bartender said.

"Depends on what you mean by work," I said. "If you like to cook, there's no such thing as too much of it. If you don't like to cook you got no right to be one."

"Gee, you're a real wolf, ain't you?" says the brunette to Joe.

"Aw listen, Darlene," says Joe.

And the bartender commenced telling me thirty different kinds of biscuits he was master of, including Calumet Quick Risers and "parking house."

It always seemed a shame to me that we had to stop so short of St. Louis, and I wished we were going down to drydock this time. We would go past Burlington Elevator and through Eads Bridge and way on down past the steamboat landing to the drydock at Carondelet. Then there was always a lot of excitement around the shipyard, with welders climbing all over the boat, boys from the shore crew drinking coffee in the galley, and maybe another towboat tied up that you could go over and visit and exchange complaints with the crew. And at night a Broadway streetcar would take you uptown in about half an hour, to the big hotels, the night ball games at Sportsman's Park, and the big movie palaces with name band stage shows. A big dirty city is better than a technicolor sunrise out in the sticks, no matter how many songbirds are tweeting. In the city you may feel lost, but you also figure you're not missing anything.

"What makes you so sure we're going over to my place?" says the brunette.

"Aw don't be like that, baby," says Joe, opening another deck of Marvels.

Meanwhile our towboat, our home, lay up at the landing by the River Transit Lime Co., with the Diesel engines shut down and the engine room strangely quiet. And the rock crusher alongside the landing was tossing up clouds of gritty white dust that settled on the leaves of the box elder trees and sifted into the deckhands' greasy collars.

Joe and I had got a break on this landing. We went off watch just as we were tying up the empties. That meant the other watch had to strip all the heavy rigging off the empties, and start carrying out rigging to the new barges we would take upriver. "We really stuck it into them other boys this time," Joe said as we were walking back over the empties to the boat. Al, the Mate, was just coming up the tow knees, pulling on his gauntlets. "Good afternoon, Alphonse," Joe said. "Let me call your attention to them interesting barges full of coal laying over there by the tipple. Now while me and Bill get into our perfumed pants and spend the afternoon uptown with some cold bottles and hot tomatoes, will you please make up them loads for us with double-up couplings?" "Go way from me, boy," said Al. After nursing thirteen empties all the way from the Twin Cities, he now had to spend our one afternoon off in fifteen days out among the sizzling coal piles while the other watch were uptown with their hair slick and with cold, refreshing, strength-building, healthful bottles full of beer in their hands. Well, here we were. And six o'clock was not too far off.

"Not only that," said the bartender, peering into his glass as though the list of his talents was to be found in the foamy Griesedieck, "but I got a receipt for meat loaf that will drive them steamboaters crazy."

"That won't be hard," said the brunette. "They're most of them that way already."

"You don't have to be crazy to work on a towboat," Joe said, "but it sure helps." This jest loses some of its punch by being repeated fifty times an hour on the boats.

"Aw now, don't talk about yourself that way," the brunette said. She really had an excellent pair of beauts, nice lovey brown eyes, and very thrilling legs, with criss-cross straps to her shoes. I seemed to see her on this summer day stretched out all white on the bed, with her long hair falling back over the edge, the St. Louis radio station playing "Les Millions d'Harlequin," and an overturned high-ball glass on the carpet.

"Look, buddy," I said, "I can't line up a job for you. Go to the office in St. Louis." I am always getting trapped at a bar by some sad apple who wants information, sympathy, fifty cents, encouragement, matches, introductions, cigarette papers or three cheers. This guy looked to me like a typical grease style cook, anyway.

I shoved my glass over for a repeater. When I thought of those poor bastards up at the landing rassling all that rigging around I felt good. When I felt good I had a drink, and then I felt better and wanted another. I always felt better and better and I never wanted to bust up the furniture like Cy Neumeister at home, who was always going to parties and after a few he would start whacking the piano with a chair or go for the plate-glass window with the fire tongs — another one of Jefferson Schwartz's side-kicks, what a boy that Cy was.

The brunette took a trip to the rear.

"Well, are we fixed?" I said.

"We got to meet her girl friend over at some sweet shop

or other. We'll get a fifth here, and some sour we can get at the grocery store on the way."

"What did she say about this girl friend?"

"Just that she was a girl."

"It's a relief to know she ain't a boy," I said.

We got a fifth of Kinsey Gold Label wrapped up in a newspaper, and the bartender set up a couple.

"I hope she won't turn out like the one in Red Wing," I said.

"Say, she was a little out of your weight class, at that," said Joe, tossing down his shot like Tom Mix.

"With coaching," I said, "she could have made left tackle at Muhlenberg."

"Where's that at?"

"Right across the street from the German Bank."

"Funny, ain't you?"

"Pretty soon there is going to be an ugly rumor going around western Illinois that I'm drunk."

"I'm feeling a little warm myself," said Joe.

*So I says, "Choose your partners, folks, here
we come to the tunnel."*

— DON DIXON

4

WHAT I really wanted to do was to slump in the
darkness at some convenient show and watch Cary Grant
light cigarettes or William Powell raise his eyebrows. I
wanted to see Merle Oberon in a big bed with silk sheets,
talking to her millionaire boy friend over an ivory plated
telephone. And where are Phyllis Haver, Laura la Plante,
and Mae Murray?

[37]

Instead of exchanging picturesque monosyllables with Joe all afternoon and wasting my talents for comedy and love on some girl with Maybelline eyes, I should have been pulling the loose ends of my personality together by studying Clive Brook's manner of manipulating a siphon bottle, further equipping myself for the stern game of life by analyzing Cagney's sneer as he grabbed tough guys by the lapels and smashed his fist into their faces. For an afternoon, for this one hopelessly paralyzed afternoon, I should have slipped under the marquee and inside to rejoin my former boy and girl friends in a paradise of silver trays, crystal cocktail glasses, and swishy taffeta skirts. But that was all so far away. I was dirty now, and my grammar was bad; I went around with bums and my girl took tickets at a movie house; I worked for wages and needed a haircut.

The trouble with steamboating is, there's too much of it. You can't get away from it. In the morning when the barges were wet with the dew and the hot cakes drowned in Karo, all good high school graduates were sitting in clean buses reading the box scores on the night games, but we were on our knees scrubbing the pilothouse floor; at noon, when the boys were hard at the egg salad sandwiches at Walgreen's and the girls were sipping their iced tea, we lay down in our dirty bunks to listen to the luncheon music of the Diesels; in the evening, when the marquee lights commenced to twinkle in the streets and the couples strolled past the dime store windows, we arose from our sad blankets and went at it again. And in the middle of the night, when the kids were asleep in their trundle beds,

[38]

the clock ticking in the kitchen and the mice making merry in the bread box, we were still at it, pumping the barges, painting the hold, mumbling, spitting, rolling cigarettes, wondering what was doing on Main Street, and feeling sorry for ourselves. And it was a dismal feeling when we passed some little river town in the early evening and heard a bicycle bell under the trees.

We would lie in our bunks, with the Diesels just on the other side of the bulkhead from our greasy pillows, smoking and feeling the coaly sweat trickle down our bellies, swatting flies and cussing the company. Then I would start to think of cold things to drink, starting with a lime freeze with a raspberry ice float at Schrafft's on Boylston Street, progressing to Jake Wirth's for a seidel of dark, then to Park Avenue for daiquiris, to the Polo Grounds for a bottle of Jacob Ruppert's, to Revere Beach for an icy bottle of "orange tonic, gents," to St. Moritz for Martinis, to Harry's New York Bar for a highball, to Dominick's Pool for spring water in a tin cup, back to Boston for a half-and-half, and perhaps to my brother Herb's for his latest concoction. After I had refreshed myself on some of these cooling draughts, I would attend a few garden parties and tea dances, where all the boys smelled of after-shave lotion and none of them had ever heard of a mop bucket, and then I would sink into a restless itchy sleep while the flies played association football on my nose.

Living this way for weeks at a time, I really owed myself a complete change of scene and dialogue. The movies. But here I was, and in my hour of greatest need what was billed at the moving pictures for the matinee? Was it a revival in which we would see Valentino as Julio make love to Alice Terry? No, it was Frankie Darro in *Tough to Handle* plus Bugs Bunny.

"What say we shove outa this mill?" Joe said when Darlene came back.

Girls, god how I love them. This one looked so nice, stood so straight.

"OK, hero," she said.

"Darlene, this here is Bill," Joe said.

"Hello, Billy Boy," she says, and comes over and plants a big smooch on me.

"Hey," says Joe.

"Thanks," I said. "That's a nice custom."

"Come on, drunk," Joe said and picked the bottle off the bar. "You'll be kissing the bartender next."

"My god it's gonna be hot when we hit the street," she replied.

"It ain't gonna have nothing on you then," Joe said.

Outside it was like standing between the boilers on the steamer *Mackenzie*. Not much doing up and down the line — a couple of beer trucks up from St. Louis unloading, some empty ice cream cones on the sidewalk.

"What's your girl friend's name?" I said.

"Her name is Toots," she said.

"The last girl I knew by that name weighed a hundred and sixty-five stripped," I said.

"You should of left her clothes on," she said.

Maybe I would have been better off at *Tough to Handle* after all. This Toots would probably turn out to be one of these cuddle bunnies with a baby voice who is all the time chewing Teaberry. I felt a stomach-ache coming on.

"She's a blonde," Darlene said.

A drugstore blonde, I bet. I don't like blondes anyway. The only blonde I ever cared for was from Chicago and she married another girl and they went to live in California.

"Is she as easy to look at as you?" I asked.

"Hell no, that's impossible," she said, laughing and nudging Joe.

"Ouch, cut that out," Joe said.

"Say, what's the matter with you, hero?" she said. "Need some Pep tablets?"

"No, I don't need no Pep tablets," he said. "Let's quit horsing around and get over to your place and I'll show you."

"Always thinking of something to eat," she said.

Again I commenced to think about my true love in St. Paul. Of taxicab rides back to the frame apartment house where she lived, of the white gloves she wore one time when we were in a streetcar, of the way it was when we were dancing, of the way she laughed and said, "Oh, you're so crazy," of the hotel rental radio still playing, forgotten, while she and I whispered together, of the steamboat whistles in the night, blowing for the drawbridge as we lay together speechless, of walking in the park, of her eyes above the sirloin steaks when we were eating at 1 A.M. in some old-fashioned café, of the flower in her hair one night, of her voice from the iron range saying "Yes, oh yes, yes I do . . ." of her arms around my neck, of her wrists and hands, of her fur coat, of her tears on my cheek, and of her black hair on the pillow when she said "I love you something awful, Bill."

But now nothing mattered, least of all love; the heat and the whiskey had me licked, so stop the violin music and take the potted palms away, and lead me to a girl named Toots. I don't care if Toots is four feet square and has a voice like a train whistle — I want a girl to talk to, a girl from Alton or a girl from St. Genevieve, from Cap au Gris or Golden Eagle, something fifteen years old from Carondelet, something in a ninety-eight-cent percale dress from Crystal City, most any kind, even one from Herculaneum, Mo.

"Here we are," Darlene said, and steered us into a sweet shop.

"That's the question," Joe said. "Where are we?"

It was cool in there, one of those places with colored glass lights in the booths. As you sat there fingering the sticky menu you would expect Charles Ray to be playing at the Bijou. We sat down in a booth. The whole place smelled of divinity fudge.

"What the hell does your girl friend want to meet you in a dump like this for?" said Joe. "I suppose she is just crazy for them double marshmallow sundaes with mashed hickory nuts."

"She don't like to come into a bar alone," Darlene said. She took a cherry coke, for booth rent.

"Oh, one a them kind," said Joe, giving Darlene a little feel under the table.

"Oh my," she said.

I was feeling worse again. I felt I might die before sunset and I was thinking how sad everybody would be at my funeral.

"Hello honey," Darlene said. "Come on in and lie down."

Say boys, here's something to look at in your Seebackroscope, a blonde, she looks like she's on the tennis team, and she's blushing.

"Golly, I thought you was going to be alone," she said, looking at Darlene and not looking at us, especially me.

"I am — practically alone," Darlene said.

"Hello beautiful," Joe said. "Come on, sit down and wiggle."

"I don't think I like you," Toots said.

"Sit down, Toots," I said.

She was in a white dress that buttoned down the front, and her legs were wonderful.

"Come on, sit down," I said. She sat down beside me.

"This here with the curly hair is Joe, honey, and that cutie with the mustache is Bill," Darlene said. "They work on them steamboats."

"Oh my god," Toots said and looked at me for the first time. "On the river."

"Not on the Atlantic Ocean," Joe said, "but on the Mississippi River. You prob'ly seen it already on picture postcards."

"Your friend is a great comic, ain't he?" Toots said to me.

"A natural born entertainer," I said. "He keeps us all in stitches."

[43]

She was such a sweet-looking thing I could have just sat and drunk milk and looked at her for a week.

"Say," I said, "you look like you thought I was going to bite you."

"I ain't afraid of you, if that's what you mean," she said, giving me a treatment with those blue eyes.

"Good, that leaves just me that's scared to death," I said.

"How come you talk so funny?" she said, lighting up a cigarette and blowing smoke in my eye. "You come from Chicago?"

"Sure, he comes from Chicago," Joe said.

"No, I don't. I was born and raised in Ioway," I said.

"You ack more like Chicago to me," she said.

"OK, OK, I live in Chicago," I said. "Right on Michigan Boulevard. I got a penthouse so I can lay in bed and see clear to Muskegon. All my meals are delivered by airplane."

"Don't think he's kidding," Joe said. "This boy of mine been everyplace."

"You're kinda funny," Toots said to me.

"Leave go my leg," Darlene said, giving Joe a shove.

"Oh my you're pretty," I said to Toots.

"How come you wear that mustache?" she said.

"Let's get out of here before one of them nut sundaes over there explodes," Joe said.

Again we struggled through the overheated streets, a handsome quartet of young people on their way to private quarters to try to make something out of the afternoon. Someday I'll see Joe in Winona or someplace and I'll say, "Remember that afternoon in Alton when we went up to

Darlene's flat?" and he'll say, "Yeah, that was the hottest day of the summer. It was 104 that afternoon." And that's all. Ozymandias.

Up a side street we climbed an outside iron staircase on an old brick building with a drugstore downstairs.

Darlene took a key out of her purse and we went into the flat.

"It ain't what you'd call cool in here," said Joe.

"No, and it's the butler's day off, too," Darlene said. "Come on, hero, get the ice out, I didn't have a drink for nearly five minutes."

They went out in the kitchen and I threw my hat on a chair and looked around at the electric-blue rayon plush couch, and a picture of some Venetian gondolas in a gold frame; beside one of these clocks disguised as a ship model with chromium sails, a soldier was giving me the big studio smile out of a glass frame. This was unquestionably the lord of the manse, and it was a safe bet he would not be home at five o'clock; he was probably sitting in some bar in Buzzards Bay or Onset drinking Pickwick Pale Ale and telling the boys about his home town.

In the bedroom there was a glass-top boudoir table and a fifteen-dollar chenille bedspread, and then there was the kitchen. And behind the kitchen was another bedroom. There were two fans moving the air around but what the hell, when it gets that hot here a fan is no help.

"Oh my god, ain't this heat awful," Toots said, falling down into a chair. "Wheeee-ew," and plucking at the front of her dress, she fanned air into her bosom.

The two front windows faced onto the street, and out-

[45]

side one of them you could see part of the electric sign for the store downstairs: D R U G S, in 40-watt bulbs. I have always thought how nice one of these places would be on a cold winter night when the wind is howling through the telephone wires and the taxicabs are all frozen up, with the store downstairs for supplies of *True Detective*, cigarettes, fudge bars, and sandwiches, and the lights on the electric sign twinkling on and off merrily, right in your window.

Well, this sure as hell was no cold winter night.

Then there were ecru lace curtains, and ash trays with "naughty nudies" on them, and a cigarette lighter in the shape of a 75mm. cannon, and for reading a choice of nine different movie magazines with intimate secrets of the stars or a new drugstore copy of *Call Her Savage*.

Joe came in with a couple of whiskeys with sour soda. He went back in the kitchen.

Toots turned on the radio and I sat down on the couch.

"Come on over on the couch," I said.

"Aw, gee, Bill," she said, "it's too hot for that stuff."

"What stuff?"

"Aw, you know."

"Come on over."

Out in the kitchen Darlene said, "Look out, crazy, you'll spill your drink," and then they went at it and all you could hear was kisses and yumyum.

"Come on over," I said.

She came over and sat down and I tipped her blond head against the back of the couch and looked into those blue eyes and said, "Let's see your tongue, honey," and she stuck her little pink tongue out a little bit and I kissed it.

[46]

Then we kissed fourteen times and I unbuttoned her dress down the front and began to get going.

"My god," I said, "what a pair." They were certainly cut along classic lines.

"Oh," said Toots. "Oh my."

Darlene came in for some cigarettes; she was in her slip with her black hair hanging down her back. With those long black silk stockings on and some creamy curves showing in the lace at the top of her slip she looked like picture #2 of a set of French postcards.

"Having fun, kiddies?" she said. "Want a nickel for some crackerjack?"

"Hey," Joe hollered from the back bedroom.

"Who you hollering *hey* at?" Darlene said watching us.

"*You*, god damn it, come on back here," Joe answered.

"Go way, Darlene," Toots said. She was undone to the panties by now. Pale blue panties at that.

Someplace a factory whistle blew for the three o'clock shift, and the sun beat down on the city harder than ever until several citizens were carried off for medical aid.

"Don't them make your mouth water, though?" Darlene said, looking at Toots.

"Aw cut the comedy, Darlene," Toots said. "Beat it."

"All right," Darlene said, and bending over with her highball glass in one hand she placed a luscious kiss. "Mmmm, strawberry," she said, and skated out to the kitchen.

Toots giggled. "Ain't she a caution though?" she said. "She'll do anything comes into her head. *She* don't care."

"Toots. Baby, let's get the hell into the bedroom," I said.

"Gee, it's too hot, Bill."

"All right, then, let's play submarine in the bathtub," I said, kissing her tummy.

"Oh my," she said. "Get me a drink. With a big slug in it."

"All right, sweetheart," I said. "But it breaks my heart to leave you for so long."

When I came back she was running water in the tub and then we played games in the tub for a while. This was the first time I had been cool in several days. I went out to the kitchen to get a couple more drinks, dripping water as I went. Joe and Darlene were talking in the back bedroom. I got the drinks and took them back to the bathroom.

"Come on," I said, and I picked her up and carried her into the bedroom and dumped her on the fluffy white chenille.

"You still think it's too hot?" I said.

"Oh, Bill," she said, kissing me like she meant it.

What of it, if some old hunks of a sea-captain
orders me to get a broom and sweep down the
decks? What does that indignity amount to,
weighed, I mean, in the scales of the New
Testament? Who is not a slave? Tell me that.
— HERMAN MELVILLE

5

TOOTS cried, Darlene cried; they suggested getting big thick steaks, going dancing, the movies, playing
cards and drinking beer, the carnival, a nice walk, more
love. But we had to go. If you work on the river you always
have to go back to it when you least want to. We made it
back to the landing in a cab with no shock absorbers and

got into our dirty clothes by quarter to six, just in time for a cup of coffee and a couple of hot biscuits out of the galley.

"Well," Joe said to Al, the Mate, when we got out on the foredeck, "couldn't you at least of got them groceries aboard in the last six hours while we was uptown?"

"Listen, buddy," Al said, "I got everything out there on that tow for you except a case of cold beer and a pillow. I got all the ratchets out, all the wires, and the long wires, and the lines, and the chains and the axes and toothpicks. And we got the engine room stores aboard, too. Now if you'll excuse me, I have an appointment uptown with four girls from Paramount Pictures."

"Where you going?" Joe said, as Al jumped down the plank and took off for town.

"I ain't going to church," Al said.

"Give it a push for me," Joe said.

We were tied up next to a rocky bank and up at the top of the bank was our grocery order, over a nine-hundred-dollar order to load.

"Look at all those spuds," I said.

"I'll carry the corn flakes," Shorty said.

"Chewing it over ain't going to make it, boys. Let's get started." Joe picked up a sack of flour and a case of Carnation and we commenced carrying our food aboard, down the rocks and up the plank, and along the starboard guard, to the galley on the stern.

"I wish Darlene and Toots could see us now," I said, following Joe with a crate of oranges on my shoulder.

"I wished I could see them," he said.

"Them must of been some girls youse met," said Shorty, coming up behind me with a couple of watermelons and a jug of syrup. Shorty was from Beardstown. Ever hear of Beardstown? It's up the Illinois River and most of the people are catfish. The rest are fishermen or steamboaters. Most of the gang in first grade have a Pilot's License, and without you have at least a Non-Condensing Steam License the authorities withhold the eighth-grade diploma.

"Mine could do everything but make it talk," I said.

"Listen what the boy says," Joe said.

"What color was she, blond or brunet?" Shorty said.

"Parts of her were white and others were pink," I said.

"Good god," said Joe.

Captain came out on the bridge beside the pilothouse and leaned over the rail.

"What's the matter with the big Second Mate tonight?" he hollered down. "Joe, you look all beat out."

"You tell 'em, I stutter, Cap," Joe said, coming down the bank with a quarter of beef.

"Why don't you take after Bill, there, Joe? Now Bill he wouldn't go to work and drink whiskey and smell around none of them town girls, would you, Bill?"

"God forbid, Cap," I said.

"Now take Diamond. He slept all afternoon and is just ararin to go, ain't you Diamond?" Diamond was the other deckhand, the one who had showed me how to splice.

"Yes sir, you bet." He never went uptown, said he didn't care to go up and fool his money away and would one of us bring him a carton of Marvels. He was saving to buy some chickens or some such project and there were always copies of the *Poultry Journal* in his bunk with articles on how to make Buff Orpingtons squirt eggs like a machine gun.

We went on down the guard and Diamond said to me, "Sure, I had a dandy sleep, with them engineers swatting the engines with twenty-pound sledge hammers and bouncing forty-eight-inch Stillson wrenches offn them steel decks. Sure, I had a dandy sleep." He dropped a case of Karo, picked it up again, and it commenced to drip. "That's right, go ahead and leak," he said.

Diamond was the well-dressed deckhand. He parted his rather greasy, silent-movie style hair carefully in the middle, and his jeans were always clean. His toes never stuck out of his socks because he did his own darning. He worked just as hard but he never seemed to get all smeared up with grease, coal dust, and red lead like the rest of us. He was about my height (they call me "average"), and he had an expressionless face that you couldn't remember when you got to thinking about him later on. And Diamond seemed to have a master plan all set up and covering his whole life, whereas the rest of us had no plans extending any farther into the future than supper time.

It was a little bit heavy loading the stores, especially the sacks of potatoes, but on the other hand the smells that went with this job were all home smells, not steamboat smells. The smell of the cases made you think at once of the grocery store you went to as a kid with a penny for one of those wax bottles with red syrup in them. As a matter of fact our grocery store at home even carried baled hay and straw. My brother Herb got some once for his rabbits. His rabbits were not very profitable and he was unable to buy the Briggs and Stratton motor wheel he had planned on.

"Oh, you morphidite," Joe said as the end of a case he was carrying gave way and cans of peas commenced to drop to the deck and roll around. One rolled off into the river, *plunk!*

Oh it was nice to wrap your arms around cases of canned peaches, chickens, baked beans, chili sticks, plums, cream style corn, sockeye salmon, halves of apricots in heavy syrup, tomato paste in little round cans, or Pulaski sauerkraut; you were not doing this for somebody else, you were taking these things back to the cook so he could cook them up for you to eat. One thing about it, we had a cook who wasn't shy at ordering. We carried the damnedest assortment of food aboard that old tugboat — sardines, pineapple, liederkranz, pork sausage, salami, strawberry preserves, lemon extract, black-eye peas, pickled herring, brown sugar, picnic slices, brick cheese, mayonnaise, grape juice, lunch meats, plum butter, clover honey, smelts, store cookies, vanilla extract, sweet rolls, spareribs, muskmelons, pigs' feet, Mapeline, Salada tea, pie apples, red grapes, watermelons, youngberries, iceberg lettuce, long johns, Postum, celery salt, bulieners, Clabber Girl, hot relish, Indian pudding — only thing missing was pickled eggs and Major Grey's chutney.

Now evening was coming. Captain couldn't think of any more funny remarks.

"Leave me know when you're ready to get at them loads,"

he hollered down to Joe, and went into the pilothouse and started to read *Real Detective*.

We went on loading. The sun was well down over in Missouri; we were working slow and steady and enjoying ourselves, and feeling the whiskey coming out in our hair.

"Aah, holy catfish, look at that," Shorty said. A couple of boys went by in a nice Chris-Craft runabout with two queens in bathing suits sitting on the hatch cover and displaying everything but the Grand Canyon of the Colorado. "The way them rich people live," he said.

"They're not rich, they're just smart," I said. "They could pick up a job like that secondhand for six hundred bucks."

"That's what I say, rich bastards."

"They look like shoe store clerks to me," I said.

Shorty picked up a case of Kitchen Klenzer and I followed along behind with a bag of onions and two jugs of vinegar. A breeze was coming up, a very light breeze from down below, and the nighthawks were beginning to show up, peeping, swooping, and climbing for those sensational power dives. The last blast of the sun was on the very top of the bluff above us. I suddenly realized that I could do this forever, that I didn't necessarily have to go back to the gray flannels and cordovan shoes. It was a nice thought for sundown; I never cared to start the evening with problems.

Shorty commenced to sing:

> Oh please do to me
> What you did to Marie
> Last Saturday night,
> Saturday night.

[54]

And as we passed the engine room I joined him for the second chorus:

> I know it was real
> Cause I heard her squeal,
> Saturday night,
> Saturday night.

I put my stuff down in the galley and went into the messroom for a drink at the cooler. There was the cook with his new messboy, trying to get the stuff put away.

The cook was fat and always in his undershirt and he seemed to be sifted lightly all over with baking powder. He had been chef in a big café on Randolph Street in Chicago but now he was a steamboat cook and the Captain didn't care if he went on a three-day drunk once a month. Still he never let us forget that restaurant. ("Why the tile floor alone cost five thousand.") His nose was on the large, rubbery order, and as it was always sprinkled with baking powder it looked like some new kind of bakery goods.

"*Don't* fool with them potatoes, son," he was saying. "How many times I tell you let's get this here meat in the cold box. We got all night to stow that other truck."

"Well, where does this here stuff in cans go?" said the messboy, just out of Gasconade County and not quite used to the daylight yet.

"Oh sweet gawd, what's the use?" moaned the cook, rolling his eyes in agony. "They'll be sending me one of them pinheaded wonder midgets from Madagascar next. You just *had* to come down out of the woods and go steam-boatin."

[55]

"I never did nothing like this here before," said the kid.

"No," said the cook, "I don't suppose you never seen more than a pound of corn meal and a handful of dried beans at one time before. Thanks to my dear old mother, gawd love her, I was borned in Illinois. Come here and gimme a hand with this beef."

I went out and walked up the guard on the river side of the boat. I would have liked to be in a movie with Toots, even Rin Tin Tin, Jr. or Andy Hardy. Wouldn't it be nice, too, on the Acropolis tonight, or along the Cannebière in Marseilles? What was going on in St. Paul? Merle, certainly not thinking of me, was sitting in a booth padded with yellow leatherette while a commercial traveler in the hardware game described the discount policy of the firm. When she smiled you could hear the angels sing, and not like the Andrews sisters, either.

"I love you, baby," I said. "Don't give that son of a bitch a thing."

"What's the matter, Bill? You look kinda sad," Joe said when I got back on the foredeck again.

"Feeling sorry for myself, Joe. Guess I got a hangover," I said, lighting a cigarette. "See the new messboy?"

"I seen him. A forty-miler if I ever seen one. By the time we get to Rock Island lock he'll decide he's got to go home to help get the hay in or breed the bull or plow the back forty. I seen his brand a many times before."

Joe sat on the double bitts and rolled a cigarette out of Duke's Mixture. Diamond sat on the bottom step of the starboard tow knee and looked neutral. Shorty was getting into a life jacket to start making up tow.

[56]

"I wonder what the stockholders are doing tonight," Joe said.

"Eating cold lobster, every last one of them," I said.

"What's that?" Shorty said.

"Kind of like channel cat only more on the order of wild rabbit," I said.

"My uncle he won't eat rabbit," Shorty said.

"No? Why not?" Joe asked, looking up at the evening sky.

"He don't like it."

"Say, that's quite an interesting story about your uncle," I said.

Shorty looked pleased. "He don't eat no tomatoes neither."

"Don't like them, neither, I suppose," Joe said, following a nighthawk with his eyes and waiting for him to dive.

"He claims they're poison," Shorty said. "My uncle says most of the people that dies dies from tomatoes and don't know it."

"Let's make up the tow," Diamond said, "and get it over."

"What's this uncle's name, anyways?" Joe said.

"Randolph, Jacob Randolph. I'm named after him. Down at Beardstown they all call me Randolph. Nobody calls me Shorty at home. They all call me Randolph. They always just call me Shorty out here on the boats."

"My uncle had a Stanley Steamer in 1909," Joe said. "He run the son of a bitch right through a grocery store, in through the plate glass and out the back wall."

"My uncle got shot to death by machine gun in a drug-

[57]

store in Berwyn, Illinois," I said. (That was Papa's brother Dude.)

Joe got up and put on his gauntlets.

"We ain't gonna cut it this way," Joe said. "We ain't making the Inland Barge Line no money setting here."

"That would just bust my heart if they didn't make no money offn us for ten minutes," Shorty said, getting up.

"Bill, you go out on the loads with these guys and see what Al's got laid out for us. I'll go up and interview Captain James E. Sargent what we're gonna do with them barges."

We climbed the bank.

"Your uncle really get shot by machine gun?" Diamond said.

"Yes," I said. "He really did."

*"Where all the nigger cat houses?" I says to
her. "White Boy," she says, "you off the river
ain't you?" I said yes and she says, "Boy when
we hears that whistle blow all us nigger gals
just back into the hills about five miles. We
even locks the dogs up." "Well god damn,"
I says, "ain't that one for the calendar."*

— THE ENGINEER

6

SHORTY and Diamond and I trudged along the
bank through the cinders and sandburs.

"Ouch! Oh, them useless burs," Shorty said, stopping to
pick them off his blue random-mix socks.

About a hundred yards upstream our eight barges were
tied off below the tipple, lying there very quiet and sub-

[59]

dued, each loaded with nearly a thousand tons of Central Illinois coal. It was up to us to get behind this dead weight and shove it 640 miles upstream. But first we had to lace our fleet together with chains, cables, and screw ratchets until all eight barges were one solid, integrated, inseparable unit.

"Do you know anything about chickens, Bill?" Diamond said. "Did you ever study animal diseases when you was in college?"

"No," I said. "If there is any subject with any practical use to it you can bet I didn't learn a thing about it down there."

I like coal. I like a beautiful big river barge piled full of it. It is black, greasy, real — it almost looks good enough to eat — but it doesn't really taste good. If it were rare, coal would make nice jewelry. After a rain the coal in the barge has a special smell. In the winter the snow settles on the symmetrical peaks, cols, *couloirs*, chimneys, slopes and crevasses, making scale-model mountain ranges in the barges. I have towed a lot of fuel oil, gasoline, and Bunker C, but there's no charm in petroleum, just a continuous sickening smell.

"How come you never learned nothing?" Diamond said.

"I didn't say I didn't learn nothing. As a matter of fact I learned everything. But not about poultry lice."

"The first thing to do with chickens," Shorty said, taking his Black Sea cigarette papers out of his cap, "is to leave raising them alone. There ain't a cent of money in it."

"Aah, stick to the corn and hogs. You know as much about chickens as you do about Paris France."

[60]

"All right. You'll remember what I said someday."

There were a couple of big 235-foot Federal barges against the bank, with our barges hanging outside them. We climbed up on the Federals and walked across the deck onto our loads. I looked over the rigging the other watch had left for us. Diamond and Shorty kicked idly at the rigging and argued. Sometimes I got sick of listening to it all. Their conversation and phrasing seemed overripe. I could see some eager student of Americana in a homespun tie and needing the clippers up the neck taking it all down with enthusiasm in a ring-binder notebook.

Toots. I wanted to think more about that instead. If she had gone to the movie as planned, she was wiggling her soft creamy bottom on a velours seat and giving a Clark bar some experimental love bites with those sharp little white teeth, whose marks I could feel on my shoulder under the chambray. The prospect of nightfall was now immediate. I wanted to run up the tracks to town and grab Toots — up in town where the street lights burn all night and it never gets dark.

But the river was running down on the outside of the barge fleet — cool in the evening shadows, with a little drift from out of the Illinois River — sticks, bottom-land trash, a split fence post, once in a while a bottle with the label washed off. A lot of that slowly passing river had made the trip down from the Twin Cities, too, and that set me to thinking of the new trip we were about to embark on, and of my steam-heated Cinderella at the end of the line. One afternoon or evening soon, we would creep into St. Paul past the slaughterhouses, tie off our coal, and that evening I would find myself in an alley or on a rooftop with Merle biting my lower lip. Boys, she was beautiful and passionate and grownup. And love will rule the world.

"Why don't you guys abandon that comical minstrel show argument and help me straighten out this rigging?" I said.

"If there was money in chickens then why did Rockefeller go into banking? Why didn't he get himself a dozen Plymouth Rocks instead?" Shorty said.

"Oh hell, leave it go," I said. "Look at all the rigging the boys got out here for us. All we got to do is make 'em up."

"Sure, all we got to do is make 'em up," said Shorty, sitting down on a timberhead. "Wait till Joe gets up here from the boat and we'll find we got to poke this here number 30 around the head, move about twenty barges to get it there, drop number 19 behind 112, turn 'em around a few times, set number 9 on the other side, then bring it back, drop 108 back to the stern and put it where 111 is because Cap don't like the way they got it loaded, and then tie 'em off and spot empties for two hours. After that we'll prob'ly find that we got to move them Federals to St. Louie so they won't go aground tonight."

"Diamond," I said to the poultry king, "did you ever hear one deckhand that could moan and groan as much as this boy from Beardstown?"

Joe came across the deck of the Federal.

"Here comes the Chief High Second Mate, boys," said Shorty so Joe could hear him. "Let's all get some big smiles on."

[62]

"Ain't this calm, peaceful atmosphere got you cheered up none yet? Man, you sure got them evening blues," said Joe, and he took off his cap with the star on it and ran his fingers through his streaked blond hair.

"All right, boys, here's the way she looks," he said, concentrating and looking around him at the barges. "They got 108 and 111 all jockeyed up and ready to face up to. Now they got all our rigging right here for us, must of brought the boat alongside and throwed it off. First we make the coupling here between 111 and 16. That's 112 ahead of 16, and we got to yank her out and set her in here where 30 sets. We'll let 9 that's up on the head flop around on the outside of 30, hang the both of them on the head, and we got her made, slick as a Rock Island whore and twice as cheap. Run them ratchets out, boys. St. Paul here we come."

Down on the boat the Captain tossed *Real Detective* off the bridge into the river, went into the pilothouse and turned on the radio, shoved the windows back further, stuck his head out and hollered down to the Chief Engineer, who was taking the evening air leaning against the capstan: "Hey Curly, all them deckhands are up on the tow. Turn her loose for me, will you, and we'll shove up alongside."

"Sure y'all don't want me to come up and tie your shoelace, too?" The Chief was from down in the big bends and tall timber around Wolf Creek, Ohio River, off those big tows out of Pittsburgh, and this Upper Mississippi stuff was beneath him. He was a 250-pounder with steel-rim glasses, a tan company uniform, and an unlimited tonnage license on both Diesel and steam. All his conversation was complaints or sarcasm.

The Captain shoved the indicator to SLOW AHEAD, to hold the boat against the bank, while the Chief climbed up the rocks to turn her loose. Captain Sargent picked up the log book, which had LEDGER printed on the front, and wrote:

> 8:35 Mile 204.2 Finished taking on stores. Commence
> to make tow 8 loads.

"Another day," he probably said to himself, watching the Chief, who had got the line loose and was pulling it aboard with the capstan. I suppose he was wondering what his wife and the kids were doing, and whether the chickens were laying good.

Shorty and I took one side and Joe and Diamond the other, got our single wires on and were doubling up our long wires when the boat came up alongside the barges, dead slow, with the guard lights on, quiet except for the generator that was running wild as always.

The heat of the day returned as a slow breeze came up from the south, bringing with it evening scents from the street corners of St. Louis mixed with the sweet vegetable smell of the islands and Anheuser-Busch.

I took off my shirt and tossed it under the coaming.

"Let's go up and get number 9 swinging, hey, Cap?" Joe hollered up into the bugs and dark. "If he'd turn that radio off maybe we could get this here mess made up before the ice comes in," he said to Diamond. "Bill, go on up on the head of 9 and stand by to turn the side line loose.

All right, Jim, *Let's go*," he hollered up at the Captain again.

Sargent turned off the box and settled down to work.

Rusty and Vincent, the Junior Engineer and the striker, standing on the steel plates between the big Superiors, took off their shirts and got ready to answer the indicator. The Chief strolled through the engine room, wiped his face on his handkerchief, and retreated again to the deck, where he settled on the companionway steps and said to himself, "Boy oh boy, look at them pore foolish deckhands sweat and strain."

Making tow can be easy if you have a good mate and a crew working together, or it can be all sweat and hard feelings. Some mates get excited, start hollering at the deckhands, get things all balled up, cuss the pilot throughout the proceedings, and end up with a deckhand in the river, another one ashore to the doctor, and everybody sore. A mate that operates on this schedule can't keep his deckhands long enough for them to learn to work together and so no improvement is ever forthcoming and life aboard, instead of being a Little Bit o' Heaven, is more on the order of getting married and going to live with ma and pa so far as peace and harmony is concerned.

Shorty and Diamond and I had worked together long enough to know who wanted the ball for a shot without calling time out for a discussion. And Joe was a mate that made everything look easy. Some of these mates have an instinct for the hard way; it is not in them to formulate anything but roundabout, obscure plans of action which confuse the deckhands and delay the performance. None of

[65]

that in Joe. He was always out in front and always using his head.

So we labored and it grew dark. Sargent helped us with the searchlight. After about forty minutes we had the barges all shuffled around and laced together with plow steel.

"Now, you bastards," Joe said, addressing the barges, "don't let me hear no more outa you until Keokuk lock."

"I believe we've got her," Diamond said.

The first time I made tow the year before I thought it would kill me. I could scarcely pick up a ratchet. Now I was strong; for the first time in my life I was really hard. I felt a lot better taking my clothes off with Merle. "Baby, you're so strong," she would say, just like in the magazines.

"We've got her, Cap!" Joe hollered. "Let's go!"

"Where's Al? Is he back yet?" Sargent called down.

Just then a cab with the horn blowing came tearing down the road and pulled up in the weeds.

"That's him now, I suppose," Joe hollered. "Dropping back!"

"OK, Joe," Sargent called out. "Dropping back."

We stood on the forward deck as we dropped down to face up to the tow, taking a quick smoke. Then the boat snuggled her blunt bow and tow knees against the barges and we set the face wires. Diamond and I put our backs into the winches. We were facing up. The new trip was ready to begin.

"Leave her go, Cap," Joe hollered up at the pilothouse, and the Captain gave a single toot on the whistle to Shorty, who was out on the head of the tow eight hundred feet away. And pretty soon we could hear Shorty's voice echo down the coal piles: "A–L–L–L G–O–N–E." We were off to the northland empire. No one saw us go, and there were no baskets of fruit or light novels from Brentano's on our bunks.

It was night and ahead of us the Mississippi River and the Illinois bluffs had disappeared. We were heading up into a black wall. Now it was up to Mr. Pilot.

"Let him sweat for a while," Diamond said.

It had been a long, long day.

The pilot far aloft in his white and green cupola leaned over the wheel and looked down — cynically, I have no doubt. All pilots, being superior beings, were proudly sophisticated.

— CHARLES EDWARD RUSSELL

7

Burt Sargent wasn't the sweating kind of pilot. Little things might drive him wild, but not the channel of the Upper Mississippi. That piece of river was his private domain. In his head he had filed away a complete history of every bar, snag, and "set" in the current from Cairo to the Falls of St. Anthony. Suppose I explain about the Captain.

I have always been a sucker for anybody who would say hello to me in a cheery voice, and as long as Captain Sargent never gave me any trouble it was hard for me to have an objective opinion on him. Joe, however, had very strict ideas about the river profession and although admiring the Captain's skill, coolness, and administrative ability, he disapproved of him: Sargent worked on the river for the money in it.

Not for love, not to get away from a virago, not for the scenery, not to defeat the draft board — no, the fact was, he worked the river because he couldn't make five hundred a month on the bank doing something else.

"Well, what's the matter with that?" I said. "That's only common sense, isn't it?"

"It's a sorry reason for being a steamboat captain. He not only don't care for steamboating any more, he's actually in misery," Joe said.

Sargent had run away from home when he was sixteen, and made his way via grim, miserable toil. Now he had everything — the engraved Master's License, the salary, the glory of command — but it had all gone sour. He was stuck.

"Sure, he's up there with a look on his face like he had a mouthful of it and no place to spit," Joe said. "I bet I could smile if I had his job."

I knew, however, that Sargent had his mind on a little frame house over in Illinois, and he could remember the damp burdock leaves out behind the shed, the fresh-cut grass in the side yard in the evening, and the smoke of fried potatoes drifting under the elms on the sticky evening breeze. On every evening watch, from six to midnight, he

thought about this frame house and its contents as he sat
alone, and he filled the pilothouse with self-pity until it
was ankle deep and he had to have one of the deckhands
come up and sweep out.

It had all seemed like *Toby Tyler, or Ten Weeks with
the Circus* when he first ran away from that little back-
wash Illinois town twenty years before, leaving his mother
and father and brother Sam sitting in the kitchen staring
disconsolately from their rosebud plates to Kennedy's Fuel
and Ice calendar and back again.

"Jim's late tonight," said mother.

"Did you see him down at the lot, Sam?" said father,
mixing his peas into the mashed potatoes.

"I didn't see him all day," replied brother Sam, wiggling
his bare feet under the table.

"Prob'ly down playing ball again with the boys."

James didn't come in for supper that night, however,
or any other night, because he was in a Wabash box car
on a slow freight with Flea Doerner, who had already run
away from home three times. A few days later he was a
deckhand on the *Wm G Ranson*, an old high-pressure
stern-wheeler, bound for New Orleans. It was 1923 and he
was sixteen. He commenced to smoke cigarettes and wear
his cap on one side.

"New Orleans is a funny town they got the graveyard
above ground," his first letter home said. "The captain is
from Beardstown. We are laid up here for boiler inspection."

"Boiler inspection!" Poor old papa waved the letter in
protest above the pot roast.

[71]

In the years that followed, letters written carefully on ruled tablet paper arrived intermittently from strange river towns: Hastings, Golconda, Boonville, New Amsterdam, Minneiska, Saltillo, Morgantown, Caseyville, New Madrid, Cassville, Stillwater, Shawneetown, Helena, Cape Girardeau, New Boston, Camanche, Martins Ferry, Guntersville, Cumberland City, Tarentum, Alma, Bayou Sara, Grand Tower, Fountain City, as well as from St. Louis, Memphis, and Cincinnati and other places that a person had heard of before. These letters contained unfathomable statements: "We have ten standards and the fuel flat," "Our port engine ran through herself," "The river is bank full and we are double tripping," "The wickets here are all down."

Piecing together these mystic phrases, Sargent Senior, who ran a grocery store, came to some strange conclusions regarding his son's life and career, and since the only river boat he had ever seen was an excursion boat on the Illinois River ten years before over at Pekin, he always pictured Jim in a blue coat with wasp waist and brass buttons, his boat ablaze with colored lights from stem to stern and the steam calliope going full blast on "Danish Polka" or "Buffalo Gals."

In 1933 Jim Sargent was a sunburnt man with blue-black hair and a 24-hour-a-day ambition to advance from Mate to Pilot on a stern-wheel steamboat. Everybody considered him about 20 degrees below zero, but he was a good man to work for and he split up the dirty jobs among the deckhands so nobody got screwed. By this time he was getting so he didn't care so much for the river any more, he had had too much grief making his way, and besides, I think Sargent was never intended to get too far away from the county seat; at first the life of a wanderer had seemed exciting, but now even at the age of twenty-six he was losing interest in the big bridges and the big cities. However, he was one of these boys that want the guy's job above them; if he'd been in a pants factory he'd never been satisfied pushing an Eastman cutting machine — he'd have kept sweating until he got to be cutting fore-man, whether he liked pants or not.

Don't think this small town boy from back home didn't know what to do next on a steamboat, a fleet of barges, or in a yawl. Ten years fooling around in the deckroom and out on the barges in the rain while the boys back at the Junction were kidding the girls and imitating Monte Blue had made a steamboat man of our hero. He had been through the whole works, from A to X.

He learned to splice from a sour old deckhand from the Pittsburgh pools. ("NOT thataway, puddinhead. Watch me again.") On the Tennessee he learned to read a sounding pole on that hard sandy bottom. Peggy Bill from Trempealeau taught him how to heave the lead line, and Blackie from the St. Croix River tutored him in checking with 150 feet of line. ("You got to *feel* it, son.") And he met all the different kinds of barges, and found out all the different things you have to do to barges to keep them happy, such as sound them, pump them, calk them, paint them, sweep them — how to tie them up and turn them loose and swing them — and things not to do in connection with barges, such as fall into them when empty or under

[73]

them any time, and how to read a barge's character and determine its personality on short acquaintance.

Then there were other things he had to learn in order to be a river man: how to make strong coffee, what work shoes are the best buy, how much water to drink while making tow in July, how to get to Cincinnati from Addyston, how to drink whiskey and beer, how to scrub floors, where all the cat houses are, how to pick up a ratchet and throw a line, when to tell the pilot a joke and when to keep still, what to do when the barge pumps freeze up, how to pull a yawl, mix paint, chip, use the burning torch, splice wire, and when to look out for trouble.

Sargent was pretty happy after he got up to the pilot-house, and dollar bills were like United Cigar coupons to him; he got a gray felt hat and a fancy leather jacket and commenced paying six dollars for shoes. He kept the cleanest boat on the river and had the best delay time and accident record in the company; he loved Inland Barge and Inland Barge loved him.

And then confounding all reports on his lack of interest in women, he got married. Got married to a black-haired girl from Peoria that a mate off the Central Barge line told me used to work in one of the houses there — in fact this mate told me that's where Sargent met her, said he was working for Sargent at the time on the Illinois River. "My, but she was a byoodiful girl," he said.

"How come he married her?" I said.

"Didn't you never see Sargent's wife?" he asked. I remember this mate and I were waiting for a bus down in Carondelet when we had the conversation — it was a dismal fall afternoon — it would be ten years yet until spring.

"No, I never saw her," I said. "She came to the boat one time when I was off."

"If you seen her once you wouldn't stop to ask why he married her. She's byoodiful. And she's a *woman*. There ain't many, but she's one."

"I know what you mean," I said. Across the street was a big red schoolhouse with green window shades and the air smelled of soft coal smoke.

"You know what I mean?" he said.

"I know what you mean," I said. "All the women I know are just girls only older. They're bigger, but they aren't any better."

"They never learn nothing after they're sixteen. But a real woman gets to be more of a pleasure every year."

"So that's Sargent's wife?"

"Yeh. A woman. You know what I mean?"

So we got on the bus and went uptown and I bought a new razor at Katz's drugstore and then we went and shot some pool. This mate's name was Peaches — that's the only name I ever knew him by.

Many is the time I have brooded over the Captain's wife when I was sooging down the walls in his cabin, for her picture was on his bureau leaning against the mirror. She was beautiful, all right, although you could see that the photographer hadn't done her full justice; she was nearly as good-looking as Merle, and Merle was the most beautiful girl in the world, including outlying possessions. Sargent's wife always wrote on pink stationery and if there was a

[75]

letter on the bureau why of course I would read it, so I got
to know Marie pretty well.

Through the seasons I progressed with her from canning
to getting the boy's clothes in shape for school, then the
first snowfall and shoveling the walk, and buying stuff for
the kid's Christmas after that; in January it was the high
price of coal, drifting snow, and mumps, followed by a
rummage sale and bad colds in February, and in March
there was a hotel fire and the depot was robbed. Then came
mud in the side yard, the kid lost a front tooth, and after
planting the garden there was the Sunday school picnic
and then school was over and it was Fourth of July and
so back to canning.

"Put up sixteen quarts today. Ray helped quite a bit.
The new stove sure is swell."

She had a fur coat, and a car, and went to the Baptist
church and read ladies' magazines on how to make your
own slipcovers, while Sargent, having lost all interest in
steamboating, paced up and down in the pilothouse thinking of Marie and the kid and the baby and looking at the
Mississippi River in a very unfriendly way.

"What's the matter with the Captain makes him so
nervous?" I asked Joe when I first came on the boat.

"He's tired of it. He wants to go home," Joe said.

"What's the big attraction at home?" I said.

"Wife, kids, chickens, tomato plants, home-baked bread,
front porch."

So this was Sargent when I first met him, a homesick
steamboat captain wearing a cap like Conrad Nagel. For
shore he still favored the gray felt, for the boat it was this

Nagel type cap. Absolutely impassive in the face of possible marine disaster, he would go up like a skyrocket if the messboy dropped a plate. And he was very downcast by drownings.

"Man, the way he carried on the time that fishhead from Nauvoo got himself drowned," Joe said one time. "I been in on six drowndings already and I never seen anybody work himself up so over it."

"Sure," I said. "He gets hell from the office when a thing like that happens. Spoils his precious record."

"No, no, it ain't that. He just broods over it. It bothers him."

"I'd like to see him bothered just once."

"I come up to the pilothouse one night. 'What's the matter, Jim?' I says. 'You look like they took your license.' 'No,' he says, 'I was just thinking about that Blair kid. There's the place up ahead there where he went down.' We was up below Kemps Landing. 'Forget it,' I says. 'It wasn't your fault he fell in the river.' 'He should never of come out steamboating,' he says. 'It never come natural to him.' 'Forget it,' I says. 'I'll bet Blair's folks didn't forget it yet,' he says. So I told him about the time my brother knocked the porch off our house with his car, but it didn't help him out none, and if I can't get a rise out of him with some foolishness nobody can."

The world is filled with people who don't like the way they are making their living and it was refreshing to discover that our own Captain Kidd would have settled gladly for a good job back home at the grain elevator. It was hard to picture him singing comical songs to the tune of "Tip-

[77]

perary" down at the Rotary Club, but I have got past the point where life any longer holds any surprises.

"Joe tells me you been to college," he said to me once when we were coming down through Dark Slough in an 11 P.M. gale. "What's a smart guy like you doing out here on the river?"

"I'm not smart," I said, setting his coffee down on top of the radio. "That's why I'm here."

I went back to the pilothouse door and found the knob in the dark. We had a game going down in the messroom.

"Come here," he said, and I went back and stood behind him and to one side while he worked us around the bend, sliding our thirteen empties in the wind.

"Leave me give you some good advice," he said.

"What's that, Cap?" I said. How that wind rattled all the windows!

"Don't stay too long. Or someday you'll wake up and find you want to go ashore but you can't. You're no good for anything but shoving somebody else's barges up and down the river."

Well, the poor son of a bitch, I figured, let him suffer. He'll have to get out of this the best way he can.

"You're not married," he said as we went into another slide right on top of a red buoy. Why, I wouldn't be a pilot for anything.

"No," I said. He straightened her up but I wouldn't have bet a dime on our chances of getting down to Clinton lock.

"You will be," he said. "And when you are, boy, get out.

Go five hundred miles inland where you won't never hear those steamboat whistles blow."

Well, I thought, if this isn't one of the sorriest birds in history.

I finally got out of this campaign to save my soul and went back to our game.

"How's it look out there?" Joe said.

"It's a miracle we're not piled up in the rocks already," I said. "But it doesn't seem to bother him any."

"Aw, he loves a good hurricane with a fleet of empties in front of him. It keeps his mind occupied. Gimme two cards."

Sure enough, after a while we heard the whistle blow for Clinton lock, and had to get into our raincoats. One thing about the old boy, he was a lightning pilot.

This was our good Captain.

What had disconcerted Robert when his eyes
fell upon Albertine's photograph was not the
consternation of the Trojan elders when they
saw Helen go by and said: "All our misfor-
tunes are not worth a single glance from
her eyes," but the exactly opposite impression
which may be expressed by: "What, it is for
this that he has worked himself into such a
state, has grieved himself so, has done so many
idiotic things!"

— PROUST

8

In spite of delectable Toots and other such enter-
tainments, ever since the second time I saw that girl named
Merle up in St. Paul I had been running two degrees of
fever. For the first time in my life I had the genuine symptoms.

I was always a great old kid for the girls but not ac-

[81]

customed to suffering any permanent damage. I had exchanged some pretty arty correspondence in my time, but had never experienced any compulsion to hang around any one girl indefinitely, lighting her cigarettes and bringing little bunches of violets and toy bears. Every time my steam gauge would get over two hundred pounds my loved one would start running down her girl friends or tell me I would look cuter with my hair parted on the other side and I would break for the fire escape. I don't have to put up with that stuff.

But this little girl had me practically tamed. If she had insisted, I think I would have gone down with her to the furniture store to pick out the dining room suite and the rugs, as well as a platform rocker for myself.

How I happened to get caught under the pile driver is a subject for endless speculation but anyway, there was Merle, a raven beauty, with a classic example of the very very faintly aquiline nose that is so popular in the French capital, and before she had finished the first whiskey *and* sour I was in bad shape. The next day I went off down the river but the symptoms increased and by the time we were back again I had got into that awful habit of daydreaming ways of making more of a hit with her.

Things turned out OK the second time I saw her. She didn't say she thought Van Johnson was cute or make suggestions about my necktie and we made some preliminary motions in the right direction.

Then when I got my ten-day leave I went to St. Paul instead of home, and I got a room and stayed there, and even after we had spent three days in bed I still loved her, which is a pretty tough test, and I was not anxious to get over to the Eagles' Hall and get in the game of rummy, but would have liked to stay on for another three days, or three years, only it got to be Monday A.M. and Merle had to comb her hair and go to her job.

Now this young lady was perfectly beautiful and she did not read *Vogue* magazine, discuss Braque, Albright or Rouault, did not have to be cajoled and flattered into bedding, or act real peppy and cute. She did not try to talk like Hepburn or to put character in her handwriting by separating all the letters, nor did she talk sexy and then run for cover when cornered. She shut up when she had nothing to say. She did not quit drinking at a party for fear she might say something natural; neither did she get drunk and blow lunch. She did not live on fruit salad and sleeping pills. If she felt like it she chewed gum. She did not claim to like or know anything about prize fighting or baseball. She did not say she wished she had time to read some really good books. She did not give a good god damn what kind of hat the girl at the next table had on. She didn't want to go to Hollywood and see the homes of the stars. And loving was her middle name.

She was about kissing height on me, and when I had my arms around her and commenced to go over the territory everything was firm and yet soft all at once. Like most females she had a mouth, but instead of using it to issue a lot of misinformation she had given it several extension courses in kissing in the international manner, and in the words of the song, when she kissed you, boy, you sure stayed kissed; her idea was neither to mash you with heavy application of pressure nor to strangle you with her tongue, and although I had put in considerable time practising since I was twelve years old, never in my exhausting career was there anything like this, even in *100 Ways of Kissing Girls*.

Then I loved her black hair, which she wore in a rather stunning way on her shoulders, and her slender hands, so adept at subtle caresses, and her throat to be kissed, and her crowning triumph, a nose so pure, so fine, of such a rare and matchless design that there never was such an admirable, passionate, and aristocratic nose anywhere, from Sioux Falls to the Persian Gulf.

But it's hard to describe a girl. I had a friend down there at school, a bird from Waynesboro, Pa., who was always describing girls in his themes and their teeth usually turned out to be "like freshly peeled almonds." I told him I had never freshly peeled an almond and what did they look like and he got mad as hell. Well, thank god Merle's teeth didn't look like almonds or any other nuts or fruits.

There seemed to be some conflict in her mind as to whether I was IT or not. There was no conflict in my mind. She was IT, all right, and I seldom stopped to think how she would fit in with Herb and the gang at home, and Papa. She would pledge undying love in the most alluring phrases from the silver screen, but she was certainly not interested in sitting around talking about hem lines with her girl friend when I was off down the river someplace near St. Louis. She had an unpleasant habit of going out with other gentlemen. One of them was a slot machine king. Another was a mechanic over at the Hudson Garage.

I didn't know whether she was giving these guys any, and it made me so sad I didn't even want to think about it.

Under the circumstances the thing to do was either see if I could get a discount on a diamond ring or else clear out. The trouble was, I didn't want to do either. Not right then. I had been out steamboating a year. I was beginning to feel more at home on the boat than on the bank, and I was already thinking about getting Mate's License.

"You bother the hell out of me, angel," I said to her.

"That's good," she said. "You bother the hell out of me, too. That's what they call love, baby."

*Ah landsman, landsman, you can make noth-
ing of this; it will be all alien and comical to
you.*

— CHARLES EDWARD RUSSELL

9

ON THE MORNING of the second day north of
Alton we met the big steamer *Mackenzie* coming down
with a whole riverful of empties in front of her and throwing smoke and cinders all over the valley like another
Pelée. "There comes the big *Mack*," Joe said, and we looked
upriver and she was coming down around a point about

[87]

a mile upstream. Our pilots exchanged whistles and when the *Mackenzie* blew we could see the plume of steam go up, and then after a few seconds the heart-rending music of a real old-time steam whistle came drifting down across the channel. Everybody on both boats knocked off when they heard the whistle, and when we came abreast the cooks waved aprons at each other, the engineers and mates saluted with varied gestures, the pilots walked over to the side of the pilothouse, slid back the windows and gave the two-handed wave, and the deckhands hollered: "Hey Creeper, whyn't ya get on a good boat!" "Hey Mush, where's Lucille at?" "Hey Dogface, how you like that fuel flat!" "Hey Smitty, where's my six bucks?" And then we were almost past, and her great big paddle wheel was alongside us splashing all wet and shiny with a rainbow in the spray, and pretty soon she was gone, away down the river, and all we could see was her wheel wash, and then she cut behind an island and her smoke on its way to heaven was all that was left.

"We had a deckhand once and he asked me to write a letter home for him. He couldn't write very good, or he couldn't write at all, one. So I got the address wrote out for him and then I says, 'All right, buddy, what shall I say?' 'Oh,' he says, 'tell 'em we ben goin up the river and now we're goin down her.' Kind of a simple description of steamboating, ain't it?"

"That just about tells it all. We ben goin down the river, and now we're goin up her."

"That's it, ain't it?"

"That's about all."

[88]

Sometimes the river would follow a course down the middle of the broad valley, and the escarpments that marked the limits of the flood plain would be a mile away on each side; the big broad stream would roll very wide and slick, on down between islands and towheads as wild as the Magdalena, with snakes and lumpy toads in the sandy scrub, redstarts and blackburnians fluttering in the pale cottonwoods, and nettles waiting. Then the channel led us close along a rock-paved bank of riprap, and we crept along the shore next to the dark jungle; backed up against the trees a government light was flashing foolishly in the morning glare, and a groundhog, come for a scenic view of the river, poked his nose through the burdock leaves and saw with his beady eyes the piles of black coal mysteriously moving past the shore.

"I grant you, it's purdy in a way, but you should see the Ohio over around New Amsterdam. And Wolf Creek. And Cave-in Rock. And Madison, Indiana. Boys, now that's really purdy country."

"I suppose they got a Lake Pepin over there. And a Queens Bluff. And a Sugar Loaf. And a Trempealeau, too."

"They don't need no Lake Pepin. They got Cincinnati and Louisville. They got Pittsburgh, and a lot of things you never even heard of."

"Too bad you hadda leave and come over here to no man's land."

Then the river would shy away from the middle of the valley and go on a long tangent full of sandbars and

[89]

wooded islands and little scraggy willow towheads over toward the Missouri side; we would run parallel to the bank now, with a hundred-car freight pounding the rails beside us so close we could bounce lumps of coal off the sides of the boxcars. And on up the shore past a deserted gray house with roses blooming among the weeds, and a Model A Ford upside down in a ditch, and a meadow lark on a fence post.

"After you get through banging them dishes together in the dishpan you can start on your beds."

"Nobody down there at St. Louis tole me I hadda make no beds on this here job."

"My that makes me sad to hear that."

"They never said nothing about no beds."

"Ain't there a nice novelty to it, though? I don't suppose you got beds down in Gasconade County."

"The hell we ain't. We got three beds right in our own house."

"My, my; you must be the rich folks in town."

"We don't live in no town. We live out on the branch, right near Gilberts Bridge."

"Leave me know when you're ready, and I'll show you just one more time how to make up them beds."

"They never said nothing about beds. I got half a notion to quit."

"Get another half notion and you'll have a whole one, and you can end your travels right up around the bend."

"Aw."

Ever so slowly we moved along, and the heat waves wiggled above the coal piles; the slow freights bound for

Hannibal shot past us like arrows. The cars on the highway burned up the slab on hot rubber, and in the little towns without curbstones the salesmen opened their sample cases: "This is one of the fastest moving numbers in the line. Try a case on consignment. 3/10 EOM. Shows you a dandy markup at 49 cents." Then the salesmen drank Cokes or Dr. Pepper and piled back into their cars and rocketed off to the next live account.

"He beat my young brother five years old so bad the kid was in the hospital for over a month. I been hunting for that son of a bitch for twenty years, and when I find him I'll kill him even if he's on his deathbed. Don't tell me about no stepfathers."

"Well, Mush, you ain't agoing to find him out here abumming on the boats."

"I'll find him."

Over it all was the sweet hot smell of the river and the islands, of the cottonwoods and wild grapes, and the rich dark mud from the north, brought down to the river by so many little creeks from the prairies. Over on the bank everybody stopped to watch the towboat go by — the kid hoeing the bean patch and the girl with red hair hanging out the wash — even the salesmen and tourists eased up on the gas for a moment to look at the clean white boat and the amazing long rows of barges stretched out in front of it, and wondered for a brief uneasy moment where we were going and whether we might not perhaps be writing up fewer orders but having more fun. The locomotive engineers pitied us because we were so slow and had no

[91]

brotherhood and a rotten wage scale; the kids envied us because we didn't have to go to Sunday school or wash our necks, and could smoke cigarettes right out in the open; and the rest of the crowd looked across the water at us with the old primitive wonder of the landsman watching a floating object move away from today and tomorrow, whether it be a drift log, a shanty boat, or the *Herzogin Cecilie* bound for Sidney.

"That's what we got that ole anvil asettin in the deck room for. That's so as when you ain't got nothin practical to do you just pick her up and hold her in your arms. Then if Captain shows up he'll see you're astrainin on somethin and he'll be satisfied."

"Well, one thing, I says, I'll guarandamtee ya I ain't agoing to wheel no mo' coal until we pumps out that fuel flat and real good."

"I tole her, I says, baby you better take a good look at the floors and the walls, cause when I gits home all you're gonna see for five days is the ceilin'."

"Yeah, well, I tole her to shove it ifn she din' like it."

"Well, after what I ben through I was as black as Coaly's ass so I didn't much care."

" 'What's ben agoing on here whiles I ben away?' she says. Why man,' she says, 'this here place looks like a Saturday night backhouse. You and them bums,' she says, 'you must have had a time of it, you got the most ornery friends of any one man I ever seen.' "

"I never did care for Caseyville. Or any other part of Kentucky for that matter. But I wished I was back there anyways. A person don't feel confortable way up here on this end of the river."

So the famous sun kept beating down from the east out of a very high, pale sky, and the morning wore along; Lake Itasca and the headwaters were still a good ways off in the direction of Winnipeg; and the forward watch were going about their business in a happy daze — even Sargent, with the pilothouse windows wide open, was gazing up the river with his idea of an agreeable expression on his face. In his room asleep, the Pilot brushed a fly off his nose and turned over. The Assistant Engineer dozed off in his bunk reading *Hunting and Fishing*, with the stump of a White Owl still in his mouth.

"We got to shut down the port engine for about half an hour."

"OK."

"How much you figure we're makin?"

"About three point four."

"Pretty good with that mess of coal."

"Yeh, we're going up the river."

"Considerin the shape we're in. By god if they don't leave us go to drydock next trip down I'm walkin offn her."

"Then you better start right now raising particular hell with the office. They sure want this here coal moved."

"We ain't agonna move nothin pretty soon lessn we go into drydock."

The messboy swept out the Mate's cabin and the Mate woke up and smoked a cigarette, squashed it out on the floor and went back to sleep. Down in the pigpen, the deck-hands off watch slept in the attitudes of the dead on the fields at Gettysburg. The cook lit a fresh cigar, pushed open the screen and stood in the doorway of the galley studying the passing shore. Up on the port side, forward, the Chief Engineer had set his poker chair on the deck and was sitting there smoking cigarettes and sucking his teeth, and in the engine room the Junior Engineer and the wiper were down behind the engines operating on a pump.

" 'There you go again,' she says, 'criticizin my brother Cletus!' 'No, I ain't criticizin,' I says. 'I only say it's funny you take him so serious, when you come right down to it he ain't held a job since 1916.' 'That's enough,' she says, 'outa you.' 'It's enough for me,' I says and I packed my suitcase. 'Good-by,' I says, 'I'm going back steamboatin.' "

Joe and Shorty and Diamond had the acetylene torch out on the foredeck, and were cutting wires, pouring dead-eyes, and trying to straighten a bent ratchet. And I was far out of sight, down in the rake compartment of the star-board lead barge — black and suffocating down there — with a flashlight and a hatchet, driving shingles into a crack in the knuckle to see if I could stop a leak. And not doing much good, either — the leak was hard to get at. As the barge breasted the current there were terrific gur-glings down there where I was, suggestive of different ad-ventures such as drowning.

"Then what did he say?"
"What could he say? Nothin."
"Then what?"
"Why this old girl says to me, 'Poor Uncle. He's better off.'

'Oh,' I says, 'are youse one of the family?' 'I'm Delbert's girl,' she says. 'My, he don't look very good, does he?' she says and leans over the coffin and feels his necktie. 'That's sure fine silk, though,' she says. I b'lieve if nobody woulda been there she'd of made off with the tie and all.'"

"Sounds like my sister-in-law from Hennepin."

"Just then in come my cousin Honey. 'He don't look very good, does he?' she says. 'No,' says the other one. 'They couldn't do nothing with his teeth.'"

Up and up, past the sweet clover blowing on the tow-heads, past the mouths of creeks overhung with drooping trees, past the cut limestone railroad stations, abandoned steamboat warehouses, birch-covered hillsides, past Clarksville and Louisiana, past Hickory Chute and Angle Island and Cincinnati Landing and Taylor Station Light, and the landsmen stand among the tiger lilies growing beside the railroad tracks and look across the water at us, and we lean against the tow knees and spit in the water moving past and look at them. Sometimes we give them a languid and condescending wave, the poor boobs, and look at their faces above the flecks of foam gliding between us on the surface of the current. And then we are moving upstream and we are under a shady point or heading up on the drawbridge, or making a long crossing over to Illinois, but the landsman is still back there looking after us; he has no desire to go and sit in the kitchen or cultivate the Kentucky wonder beans — the sight of the boat has ruined his disposition for the day. We don't even look back at him standing there in the tiger lilies by the tracks.

[95]

"When you going back?"

"Back where?"

"Back where you come from. What'd you come out here with us bums for anyways? With your line of gab you could do good at something on the bank."

"A bird named James Barrie, an Englishman, said everyman should do something, once in his life. He said he wanted to know what it was like to be really alive. He was thinking of going to the South Pole with Scott. Well, he never went, but he must of felt about the way I did back home running the furniture factory. Out here I feel like I've been dead for thirty years and just came to life."

"How about all that dough your old man spent educating you up? I'll bet he's tickled to have you out here with us wahoos, and a hundred a month."

"My old man thinks people should do what they want to do. If he'd of listened to his father he'd still be a mill hand in Lowell, Mass."

"What happened to this Scott?"

"Who?"

"This guy that was going to the South Pole. Did he make it?"

"No, he never got back."

"What happened to him?"

"What the hell you think, sunstroke? He froze to death."

"We had a farmer freeze to death up at Fountain City one winter. I seen him after they got him thawed out."

"How'd he look?"

"Punk."

Sure you can write a book. You can fly like Lindy, too.

— OVERHEARD IN A CABARET

10

THERE is always some alarming or dismal feature about every job, and in towboating on the Upper Mississippi River it is the lock at Keokuk, Iowa. This depraved lock is too short and too deep, the lockmen are more bored and obstructionist than any others, the extension guide walls are floating sheer booms that disintegrate and produce lawsuits, resignations and dementia praecox, the upper sheer fence angles off from the direction of the lock wall causing despair and vulgar language on the part of the deck crews, and it is always either raining or 400 degrees Reaumur there. When the boats leave St. Paul or St. Louis the crews begin to bet and speculate as to which watch will get stuck with Keokuk lock, and mates have been known to commit self-destruction and other acts against nature on coming on watch and seeing the familiar contours looming in the river ahead.

"We're it," said Joe as we foregathered at watch time by the engine room door, and a beautiful zigzag of lightning suitable for framing shot down through the dark clouds hanging over the willows on the Illinois side. The rain we had been expecting all day began to fall. In the steaming misty near distance we could see the black gates of Keokuk lock beyond the drawbridge, and the old wooden fence of the sheer boom floating in the water below the huge pile of concrete.

"I'm glad I greased up these oilskins," I said.

"Where's Shorty?" Joe asked.

"Back in the pigpen trying to borrow a raincoat off of Hubert," said Diamond, kicking a lump of coal in the river.

We met Al, the First Mate, coming back from the head of the tow as we dragged ourselves reluctantly out between the barges.

"Well, for once we're really stickin it to you, boys," he said. "This makes up for Alton, hey Joe?"

"How would you like to kiss my Royal American?" said Joe.

"Not much." Al went on back to the boat, and we stood around on the wet barge decks feeling sorry.

The town was close over on the port side, and we were all thinking what a good evening this would be to go to a show or out to the dance hall as we looked up at the streets and houses. We would be all evening getting our barges locked through, and with the raindrops already splashing in the river, it looked as if we were in for treatment.

Captain Sargent blew the whistle for the bridge below the lock, and after a while the big swing span commenced to wheel open, so slowly you could hardly see it move at first.

So we stood there and Sargent eased her past town and and on up toward the bridge. We could see right up the main drag. This was a sad kind of evening on the boat, with the neon lights reflected on the wet street so near at hand, a few cars so close we could hear the tire noises, and a smell of pork chops in the air. A Model A came down the street and stopped, and a girl in a blue slicker got out and ran into a store.

> Oh, please do to me
> What you did to Marie . . .

Here came Shorty along the barges, in a teamster's slouch hat that he reserved for rain. He kept his razor and tobacco in it under his bunk, between times.

"This shows the results of whiskey, women, and card playing," he said, approaching us, scuffling in the coal and shielding a cigarette as he lighted it.

[99]

"They really stuck it in and broke it off this time," I said.

"Thanks to the Lord we only got eight loads," Diamond said.

"Run back and eat a couple more eggs," I said.

"I'm gonna be wet before long," said Joe.

We could see the lockmen moving around up on top of the lock, getting ready to open the lower gates — they looked about the size of window washers way up on a building. We were right in the drawbridge now, and the lights of cars waiting in line for the bridge to close, and their suggestion of dry comfort, shows, restaurants, cocktail bars, didn't cheer us up much.

The lock blew an OK whistle at us as the big lower gates, like a pair of doors to a De Mille temple, parted in the middle and very slowly began to open in the gathering gloom.

"If that don't look like the god damn gates to hell," Joe said.

The rain came down in big drops and finally broke loose with a regular backwoods cloudburst, so we could scarcely see the gates, and Captain Sargent, four barge lengths back, could see neither the gates nor us. We were coming up dead slow.

Shorty pulled off the rake hatch cover and slid down inside, out of the rain. Joe was on the starboard corner of the lead barge looking for that floating timber sheer boom. The rain was dropping down so hard it splashed right up your legs and cuffs and found a way to get you wet in spite of the oilskins.

"There she is," Joe said. "Bill, run back a ways and

[100]

holler at Sargent the Great and tell him he cleared the sheer fence."

I trotted back and hollered up at him. He didn't hear me so I went back further and hollered some more. Finally I went clear back to the boat and climbed up to the pilothouse and told him.

"Tell Joe to tie her off if he can, until the rain leaves off," he said. "I could see a hell of a lot more if I was under a thousand ton of coal. I'll drop her against that wood boom, and be careful you don't tear nothing up."

I went down and the rain was harder yet. The wind was blowing from the east, across the water. When it first started it came straight down, but now it was beginning to slice and slash. I ran back on the port side and got an empty vinegar jug from the stern, slid into the galley and filled it with coffee about a third of the way. The cook was standing there clean and dry in his white clothes smoking a cigar.

"Why don't you just get a pail and bail the whole river into my galley?" he said.

"Aw have a heart, Harry," I said. "It's wet out there."

"Here," he said. "Put some milk in that there coffee," and he handed me a can of Carnation. "I'll leave you out a extra pie I made. Now get the hell outa my galley."

I got back in the rain again. I couldn't see much. The canvas line covers on the foredeck had blown their weights off and the coils were filled with water like little lily pools. I got back to the head of the barges all right and the tow had dropped against the floating guide fence and was still inching along upstream, but dying fast.

"If we can get two lines on her we'll stand less chance tearing up something. I'll ketch a line here and you ketch one on the quarter head, Bill, and we'll check into each other easy when she starts dropping back."

We got her tied off and a gull came and sat on top of one of the stakes they had the 40-watt bulbs strung on, and let the wind blow him around, and the rain was running off his feathers in trickles; he couldn't keep his balance — the fence was rocking back and forth — and he finally gave up and made a flop take-off and disappeared east.

"Ain't nothing much to do but set on these lines," Joe hollered. "You OK, Bill?"

"I could use a couple shots of old Peoria whiskey," I said.

"Someday I'm gonna buy me a rain outfit," Joe said.

The rain began to slack off; first we could see the big wide steps beside the lock, then the gates came into view, and the big dark lock with sheer black walls. Sargent gave a toot, meaning turn her loose, and we spun our lines off the timberheads on the fence; they lit with a splash in the river and we pulled them aboard.

"COMIN AHEAD," Joe hollered in a voice loud enough to scare the kids clear back to Canton lock, and gave a slow drag of his arm from low down in back, up over his head, and forward, like a slow-motion baseball pitch. Sargent poured it to her and we commenced moving up.

"Come on, Sargent, get the lead out," Joe said. "We ain't got all night to screw around here."

"He's probably busy listening to the Harmony Kids," I said. "Got that damn radio going again."

[102]

"Where's that coffee jug?" Joe said.

We got in the lock, and Sargent flopped the barges against the wall and they slid along slow and easy, once in a while throwing up cement dust and sparks when they rubbed the wall or hit a rough place. Cap turned the light on Joe and Joe gave him a stopping signal and we drifted for a few minutes.

"Watch your heads. Here come the lines," hollered the lockmen from way up in heaven someplace at the top of the wall and out of sight in the rain.

Diamond was back at the second coupling and I heard him holler. "OK, let her come. You can't kill me. Toss her down, old man Keokuk." Then I heard the klunk as the monkey-fist knot on the end of the heaving line hit the rake deck.

At the same time I heard another klunk only more like bouncing a baseball on a cement sidewalk, followed by a clatter of breaking glass.

"What's that? Did Shorty drop that coffee jug? Shorty!" Joe said.

Shorty was lying down in the coal as if he wanted a nap.

"He's knocked cold," I said. "Joe, here's Shorty, out like a Monday night. He got hit with the heaving line."

Shorty was lying there in the coal with his finger still through the ring on the neck of the busted jug, and his old slouch hat had rolled off and was gathering summer rain.

"Oh pretty mama," said Joe, coming across the deck. "That's what we need, a deckhand in the hospital."

I went over and bent the heaving line into our lock line while Joe was working on Shorty.

[103]

"All right, take it up!" I hollered up into the empty spaces and my voice echoed back and forth in the walls of the lock. The line arose from the deck like the Hindu rope trick and traveled up and up till the eye in it disappeared over the edge of the lock wall forty feet above.

"Shorty! Shorty you get up, hear me? Shorty you son of a bitch, get up. Ah Bill, this ole boy is cold," Joe said, shaking Shorty and banging him around. "Oh, oh. Feel that knob on his head. Now I got nobody to stand the head line."

About this time Shorty opened his eyes and said, "I knew that mule would git me someday."

"Ah," said Joe, "he's alive," and picking him up and shoving him across the deck he said, "Give him the line, Bill. Let's you and me go back and jackknife. Come on, kid."

Shorty was standing there with a dazed look on his face; he didn't know where he was but he laid the lock line around the center cavel, ran it over to the timberheads, and began to check her like an old master. Last I saw him he had a good strain on the line and was standing there bare-headed with the rain still coming down, rubbing that knot on his head and looking up at his line rising in the air.

Joe and I jackknifed and broke the couplings on the two outside barges and Sargent backed her out, leaving three in. We tied off on the sheer boom and sat down in the rain. Shorty and Diamond were up in the lock on the barges, locking through, and the rain was coming down steady.

She says "Now look what you done" and I
says "I ain't done it yet," so when I was fin-
ished she says "Now are you satisfied?" and
I says "Yes."

— A CONVERSATION ON THE MISSISSIPPI

11

"HIGHTAIL it back and get us another jug of coffee," Joe said. "I'll set here and mind the lines. I can't get no wetter regardless."

I went back to the boat and the rain was splashing all over and the smell of the breeze across the water reminded me of that place we used to go to at Riverside Gardens —

[105]

the breeze rippling the water and us lying in the sand ("Look out, lover, that sand don't feel so good when it gets in certain places"); then we would go dancing in the casino and drink Schmidt's City Club, and when they played a waltz little colored sparkles danced around the ceiling while the shuffle mingled with the saxes going goo goo goo, love me up kid I got the Limehouse Blues.

I went to the stern again to hunt up another jug, and stood there for a minute and let the rain hit me from the east and watched the cars down on the bridge, and then went in the messroom. Curly, the Engineer, was sitting there drinking coffee with soda crackers in it. Our simple messboy was talking to him and crunching an apple with his rabbit teeth.

"I use to had me a real nice guit-tar, but like a jackass I went to work and done sold it to a feller," he said.

"Directly we get to St. Paul I'm gonna go uptown and get me a new jacket," said Curly. "I'm sure tard of this here one."

"I use to play me some awful pretty tunes in that guit-tar," the messboy said. "I was a jackass to ever turn loose of it."

"Look at them sleeves, that's a fine sight for a man in my high position, ain't it?" said Curly.

"They's a knack to playin one of them ole guit-tars, but I done her real good they all said."

"I ain't agonna pay more than eight dollars for no jacket though."

"I wisht I never would of sold her."

[106]

"This here cost me six seventy-five and I ain't had her a year yet and look at the sorry shape she's in."

"I was astandin down by the store and along come Buck Rodner. 'Want to sell me that there guit-tar?' he says. 'No,' I says, 'Buck, I don't want to sell her.' 'Tell you just exactly what I'll do,' he says, 'I'll give you four bucks for her.' 'Give me the money,' I says."

These two comics would sit here chewing it over like this by the hour — they never listened to each other any more than Herb and Papa when Herb is explaining the military history of the German Empire and Papa is telling personal anecdotes from the career of Red Faber. They call it a conversation.

"What, you back again?" said the cook when I came into the galley. He was leaning against the table drinking lemon extract in milk, and the suction fan over the stove was drawing his cigar smoke out into the rainy night. "Fer god's sake don't tell me you wahoos lapped up all that coffee awready."

"The lockman hit Shorty on the head with the heaving line and when he got hit he dropped the jug on the deck," I said.

"If that blame Shorty isn't the most hard-luck son of a bitch I ever seen," he said and gave himself another tablespoonful of lemon extract. "Is he hurt bad?"

"Well, he's up there making the first locking with a lump on his head the size of a biscuit. I guess you can't kill those boys from Beardstown," I said, getting a dish of Royal Anne cherries out of the cold box.

"Them cherries cost forty-three cents a can."

"Do I look worried?" I said.

"A man must be awful hard up for work to get out in a rain like this for six hours," he said.

"Didn't you ever hear of those new social clubs they got around now called draft boards?" I said, finishing up the cherries.

"Joe is gonna get awful tired wondering where you're at in about another quarter of a minute."

"Never mind about Joe. He knows where I am."

When I got out on the head again Joe was sitting on a timberhead and the rain was not coming down in such big drops but more concentrated, like a hotel shower. The lock gates were still shut; Shorty and Diamond were tying them off on the upper sheer boom about now; one of them would stay up there to watch the loads and the other come back to help with the second locking.

It seemed like forever waiting for them to lock through and dump the water again; from the time the gates closed until they would open again to receive the second locking it was about an hour, maybe an hour and a quarter, but try sitting still or standing with nothing to do except think about how far it is to Wabash Ave. and what's doing tonight at the Aragon, with the rain coming down your neck and trickling down your backbone so it tickles and the cuffs on your gauntlet gloves wilt and crumple and the coal paste oozes in the hole in your shoe, and your cigarette falls apart and your clothes begin to smell like an old Irish wetwash without benefit of Hilex, and after ten minutes you'd swear to god you'd been in there a week and a half. It gets tiresome.

"Well," said Joe, "I still claim it's better than farming."

"Have some coffee," I said, handing him the jug.

We didn't look very romantic, dripping like a couple of muskrats in the evening gloom, even if Joe did have a star on his cap; so unless you want to take a lot of punishment, and work an eighty-four-hour week, just stick to that course in bookkeeping, boys, because you won't find any white whale out here, and the packet boats and the gamblers are all gone. So wipe off your chin and look serious and they'll give you a desk to sit at and show you how to work the water cooler and you can buy a blue serge suit and after a while get advanced from a single-tier letter basket to a double-decker. Well, I like to put on a new tie and go to the show on Saturday night as much as the next guy.

"This here is just a disease, this steamboating, a incurable disease," Joe said, and set the jug down on the deck at his feet. "There ain't hardly a man aboard that likes this here life, but they're all here to stay. Diamond is thinking about chickens. Shorty is moaning and complaining all the time worse than a Methodist preacher. The messboy wishes he had never left that red clay farm. You got that St. Paul gash and all the rest of the world's troubles on your mind. Vincent ain't hardly got the brains to be unhappy but he manages it somehow. Curly wishes he was back on the Ohio River. The cook wishes he never had quit working in that restaurant he is always raving about. And Sargent is the biggest joke of them all. He thinks he is gonna get his pile and quit. When he gets ten thousand saved up his wife will have about six operations and take up the whole wad to pay

off the hospital or the kid will come down with something
the doctors never heard of or the house will burn down,
and he'll be back setting up there in the brain box again,
and ten thousand ain't even a down payment on a good
farm these days anyways. And after a man been living on
five hunnerd a month he ain't gonna be content with what
he can make off a bunch of scabby old chickens with the
droop and the pip and pneumonia. Now his wife has a fur
coat and he has a new Chevvy at home and he really cuts
the mustard around his home town. When he goes in the
store they say, 'Well, when did you get home, Captain?
How is everything on the river? Did you have a good trip
to St. Paul this time?' *They* know he's dragging down his
five hunnerd and he is just king pin boy around that little
burg. When he goes to raising chickens and slouching
around town in a pair of dirty pants they will say 'Hi Jim'
when he comes in the store and let it go at that, and after
he loses his flock from mold or something and the Mrs.
shows up at the church supper just once in a Monkey Ward
dress instead of something new from Peoria and the other
girls give her the up and down he will shag ass for the river
like a turtle flopping off a log. I seen plenty of these smart
guys that is just out here to make their pile and they are
getting on and off these boats like they were streetcars. They
are never content again. They don't know enough to hold
down a good job on the bank. Any high school kid can slide
up Main Street and get a better job. Can't you see Sargent
striking out for a job down home? He goes to the mill.
'Well, what can you do?' says the foreman. 'Can you run a
band saw?' 'No.' 'Can you read a blueprint?' 'No.' 'Well,

what can you do?' 'Well, I got Pilot's License All Tonnage from Minneapolis to Baton Rouge and Cairo to Pittsburgh and Grafton to Chicago and Prescott to Stillwater and Kansas City to the mouth and Paducah to Sheffield and the Hennepin Canal.' 'I dunno what that's all about,' says the foreman, 'but whatever it is you better go do it.' Some kind-hearted old family friend might get him a job picking orders at the wholesale house at eighteen a week or tending bar in some slop down by the tracks, but you know what he's gonna do right now. He's gonna go to the telephone office and call St. Louis, and because they know he's a strictly fresh country egg when it comes to twisting a towboat's tail, they'll hire him back and pay his fare to Winona and in five hours he'll be down at the depot and the old lady will be bawling and he'll set in the day coach wishing to god he was dead. He got no more chance to retire from the river than a catfish has to get into the Knights of Columbus."

About this time the gates commenced to open and Diamond came down the steps from the lock and climbed over the fence and aboard the barges and I went back to see whether Cap was up and about. He was taking a nap on the bench in the pilothouse and I told him the gates were open so he blew a toot to turn loose and we shoved on up and tied off three more.

Perhaps Joe was right. Steamboating is an incurable disease, but how about railroad men — they are worse than the Jehovah's Witnesses when it comes to a one-track mind. And as for getting away from it, why Blackie Johnson quit the river and never did come back; of course, he finally got locked up at Stillwater and the problem of his triumphal return as Mate was no longer a problem to him or anyone else except the parole board. Then there was old Captain Lawrence Arkwright Buckingham who made more farewell appearances than Geraldine Farrar and after cussing the river in a squeaky voice and inadequate vocabulary for seventy years retired at the age of eighty-nine to a house-boat which he parked dangerously near the channel below the dam at Alma, Wis., so he could continue to lacerate his nerves with the passing of each boat.

After you have been on the river long enough to get the disease, everything looks different: Chicago is a town 200 miles east of the river. South Dakota is someplace west of Minneiska and of no interest as it hasn't even a mile of Mississippi River in the whole state. Lake Superior is an inferior watery deposit of some kind, in a general north-easterly direction from Grey Cloud Landing. And as for St. Louis, Quincy, Davenport, Moline, Rock Island, Dubuque, La Crosse, Winona — what are they? River towns, of course. Not towns — *river towns*. And what a difference that makes.

What possible charm can we attach to any of these towns other than that the Mississippi River flows past them, touches them? What is John Deere at Moline? French and Hecht at Davenport? Standard Lumber Co. at Dubuque? Ah, we love and cherish these mammoth enterprises because they are by the river. What is left of glamour at Reads Landing? A store with Rice Krispies — and the river. McGregor, Iowa, is all tired out but the river keeps it on the map. Lansing, Iowa, would be worse than South Dakota —

but it's on the river, and in the evening it's better than Lake Louise.

These grand old towns are pretty well shot, now. The aristocracy has fallen from the firmament and there are no bankers who read Greek in the evening. Papa and the Kellys and the Schwartzes are the new aristocracy, and they live in plastic houses with electric cocktail shakers and not a piece of reading material in sight. And the new sophistication of the inhabitants has systematically eliminated all action, drama, excitement, and color from the scene. My home town used to have a baseball team in the Mississippi Valley League and a ball park with pop vendors in lovely soiled white jackets. It's gone. We used to have an Amusement Park, a roller coaster, and a Bier-Garten. All gone. We used to have a Fair Grounds, and open-air trolleys to the scene. Gone. And a racetrack and trotting races. Gone. We used to have a millionaire who kept peacocks on the lawn, had a private trotting track, and arrived at the mill in a white suit via 1912 Mercedes limousine. Most completely gone. Why there's nothing really left there at all except the lights in front of the movie houses and 60,000 people criticizing each other and buying new-model radios. Except the river. That makes it a place. It's on the river.

Aside from the river my town is like every other American town — the fourteen-year-old girls run around Main Street half naked all summer and the evening paper is filled with sex crimes perpetrated on fourteen-year-old girls. And we have the usual town characters — a half-wit who is a scream, and a bartender who eats lighted matches; but what makes my town worth coming home to? Why, the river, naturally;

if I had lived in Fort Dodge or Topeka I wouldn't even have come home for the burial of relatives.

There isn't anything in any of these towns, but they are the most romantic and wonderful in the world because they are old Upper Mississippi River towns. Of course there's a bird in La Crosse who made a scale model of St. Patrick's Cathedral out of match sticks, a girl down in Muscatine born without any arms who can knit with her feet, and a fellow at Winona named Trask who made two holes in one, one Sunday in 1928, but those towns would be worse than Prairie City, S. Dakota, in spite of these local attractions, except for the big Mississippi River rolling past the door day and night.

Over at Indianapolis, Ind., they advertise they are the biggest city in the U.S.A. not on a navigable body of water. They don't need to advertise it — you can tell there's something wrong the minute you get there. And I'll take the Pfister in Milwaukee or the Spalding in Duluth or the Stoddard in La Crosse anyway — that Claypool Hotel in Indianapolis has a colorful name but no body of water except the municipal pool within several miles. When you get someplace where they commence to boast they got no water around it's time to buy transportation and move on.

Diamond came up to my end of the barge as we were shoving into the lock.

"Gimme the makins, Bill," he said. "I left my smokes back on the boat."

"This Keokuk is a lousy town," I said, handing over my tobacco and papers. "Were you ever uptown here?"

"Oh, it ain't so bad as all that," he said. "It's on the river anyways, ain't it?"

Diamond and I stayed in the lock to ride the barges up, and Joe stayed below with the two loads he had left and tied them off to the boom.

What time does the balloon go up?
— A SMALL-TOWN QUERY (1896)

12

THE LOWER GATES closed and there we were at the bottom of the watery pit, waiting for salvation. I was tending the lines on the forward end of the barges, and Diamond was lost down at the other end in the gloom and rain, by the lock gates. I had a lock line to the center cavel and a peg line on the quarter timberhead to keep the barge from surging, and I was thinking of the arrival of Jesus at Caesarea Philippi.

So I sang "O Zion haste thy mission high fulfilling, to tell to all the world that God is light," then switched to a lighter mood with "roll 'em girlies, roll 'em, show your pretty knees," and "when we're out in the open air the girls can't see how I learned to care but they should get him in an easy chair he's the last word," and finally they started raising the water and the barges got a little bit restless and commenced to creep up the wall.

"How you doing, Diamond," I hollered.

"Nov shmoz ka pop," he replied, or something similar. It rattled around and bounced so off the lock walls it might have been most anything.

So I dedicated a number to Merle and sang "I'll be with you in apple blossom time" with a whistling cadenza like Artie Shaw on clarinet followed by "O! Paradiso," but was awarded no contract by talent scout hidden in coal piles. I thought of my old bull terrier Max and recited a poem called "The White Cavalier" that I read one time in *Dog World,* and I thought of the time he killed Buddy Watson's police dog. "Look out for your ole dog," I told him, "ole Max is a terrible fighter." "Tell me another joke," says Buddy. "That little peanut of a dog can't fight. Anyway, a police dog can beat any other dog, everybody knows that." "Everybody but Max," I said. "You better look out," I said, "I'm not kidding." Well, of course, the police dog had to come fooling around and get tough and in four seconds or less the dogfight was on and in about thirty seconds after

[118]

that Max had Rin Tin Tin by the throat and caused a death in the family.

"Hey, Diamond, think we'll get to the top by Halloween?" I hollered.

"Wordely," he said.

We had been in there twelve years already, so it didn't much matter any more. I sang the "Freight Train Blues" for a while, and thought about whether Merle would wear the black dress, the pink sweater, or the gray suit when I met her in St. Paul, and whether I should marry her or not, and whether I would have time in St. Paul to kiss her in all the different places I wanted to. I took up the slack in my lines and gave a chorus on "My Sin," turning the clock back and finding myself in the back seat of Jeff Schwartz's 1928 Marmon phaeton with Celeste Watson's young sister Belle, both of us very flushed, tingly, and unbuttoned — "oh daddy take my garters off." After that I returned to Keokuk lock and spat on the slimy lock wall to add to the general moisture of the evening. Modern science had raised us up about twenty feet but there was more than that left to go, and whoever made the rain had sure left the faucet on.

One of the lockmen leaned over the top of the lock wall and looked down at us.

"Think it'll rain?" he hollered. A humorist.

"Hell — no," I replied. "Wrong time of year for it."

"Well, it's good for the corn," says the guy upstairs. "Been awful dry around here."

"— the corn!" Diamond hollered, making himself intelligible at last.

[119]

The lockman disappeared, his feelings hurt. I went into an Astaire routine, utilizing the timberheads, cavels, coaming, coal piles, etc. for various stunning trick effects and was working on some lyrics —

> I found you in a coal barge,
> From now on I'll really need large
> Amounts of love —

when I slipped in the wet coal and went down, getting my white flannels all dirty. A humiliating position for one of my social standing.

With all the time in the entire world available you would think I might spend some of it in contemplating The Decline of the West, Isambard Kingdom Brunel, Grants in Aid of Construction, The Implications of Boston Personal Property Trusts, The Court of the King's Bench and The Usurpation of Power of the Court of Common Pleas, Odilon Redon, Matteotti, or the vegetarian thesis for immortality; and yet never for a moment did my feeble mind ever allow itself to dwell on any except the most bestial or sentimental topics.

I remained lying in the coal, enjoying this final mortification, and singing gems from *No, No, Nanette* while the pennies from heaven splashed all around.

I had to get up and take in some more slack in the lines and I remembered one day when I was a kid I wanted some money from Papa and I went down to the old packing house, Papa's warehouse where the stuff came in from around the Twentieth Ward in Chicago. "Your papa's busy, you better not go in there," Marc said. "You better not go in there, he's got important company in there." "I gotta see him," I said. "I gotta see him right away." I wanted some money to get a new tire for my Black Beauty bike so I could go out to Fats Benedict's uncle's farm. An added attraction was that Fats's sister Geegee was coming along and I was hoping for some luscious incident. "I'm telling you, you better wait. Your papa won't like it at all," Marc said. I went in anyway, and asked Papa for a dollar and a half. There was a man in there with Papa in a gray topcoat and he said, "How old are you, sonny?" I told him and he laughed. Papa gave me a dollar and I beat it up to Meyer's bike shop to get the tire. Gosh we had a wonderful time out on the farm that day. I feel sorry for kids who never had a chance to play on the farm. And Geegee and I exchanged some of those newly invented afternoon kisses in the barn — I was crazy about her for almost a month. The next morning Papa said, "Bill, do you know who that was in my office yesterday?" and I said no. When I saw Marc I said, "Marc, who was that man in Papa's office the other day when I came down to get some money and you told me not to go in?" "Why that," Marc said, "was Mr. Torrio." "Holy smoke," I said.

Sure, Papa knew Johnny Torrio, Al and Ralph Capone, Dion O'Banion, Guinta, Drucci, and the rest of the hookup in Chicago, and my Uncle Dude was over there in a gentlemanly way handling Papa's orders and arranging the shipments. Like most of the above named, my uncle ended up with Thompson machine gun slugs in him. "Ukulele music" they called it.

I got up off the deck and took up some more slack in the

lines. They walked into O'Banion's flower shop and said hello boy and boom boom, that's all. Good-by Deany. "I think I'll buy an agency in this business," Papa said.

"By god, I believe we'll make it after all," I said to myself because we were getting somewhere near the top now, and I could see the lights in the lock house through the rain, with the rain pouring down the windows and the lights unperturbed inside; like walking down Wabash Ave. without more than two bits and looking in the windows where they are passing around those big plates of spaghetti, with meat balls.

"Hello, you meat ball," I said *sotto voce* as the fat lock tender appeared again. "Merry Christmas, you silly bastard."

"Hey, how about hauling up some slack?" he said.

"What a capital idea, old man."

We were really at the top now, and ready for the upper gate to open. Meanwhile we had to go through the inexplicable waiting period connected with getting heavy pieces of machinery to start moving. It's always the same. You blow your whistle at the bridge tender and he comes out and waves a flag and rushes back in the control house again. What does he do in the next ten minutes? Read the instruction book on how to open bridges? Get out the dental floss and give his teeth a good going over? Finish a chapter in the *Gypsy Dream Book*? Finally the bridge commences to open.

Same with the locks.

"OK on the number three," says one lockman.

"OK?"

"Yeah — OK."

Five-minute lapse.

"OK then on number three."

"OK?"

"Yeah — OK."

O'Neill should get hold of some of this dialogue.

"Oh come, oh come Emmanuel, and open those lock gates," I implored.

"How's that?" said the lockman, returning after a further exchange of OK's with the boss.

"It's a nice night for waterfowl, I said."

"I hope they enjoy it. I ain't," he replied. He was a fat goof who needed a number of pills or some Father John's Medicine from his friendly naborhood druggist. Frankly I could have used a tablespoonful of Konjola right then myself. The rain had got inside my oilskins and I was steaming inside like a baked potato. In fact I gave up in disgust and took my oilskins off finally and put them on the deck under the coaming and laid a shackle bolt on them to hold them down.

The upper gates commenced to submerge and I took up all the slack I could get and threw on some turns; the barges started to surge for the open water and the line squeaked and jumped; I checked easy and the barges gave up the idea and settled down. The lockman brought me the towing wire and I slipped it over the timberhead and after another round of OK's we commenced to creep out into the pool above. The lockman was wiping his glasses and complaining and abusing the weather department and cussing the Federal government and the state legislature; as

[123]

far as he was concerned there were no prospects in sight.

"Please Lord," I said, "bless Papa and make it rain harder. Watching this man suffer makes me forget all my sins."

"What?" he said.

"I said down on the farm they are all setting around the kitchen table listening to the radio."

He said if it didn't let up raining pretty soon he was going to tell them to take the job and shove it.

Our little game with the Keokuk lock was about over. Had I met the challenge? Had I faced up to the reality of things? Had I made myself worthy of MERLE, the beautiful ticket seller? Had I played the game or was I a rotter?

In short, the coal was on its way to St. Paul, but just where was I going, that was the question. And all the rain, what about that? What did it mean? And Johnny Torrio, how did he fit in? Was I subconsciously still in love with Belle Watson? Had I taken the right attitude with the lock tender? There I was and there was the coal and somewhere there was Merle, and there was nothing anybody could do about it. Should I marry her, or sell her to an agent exporting girls to Buenos Aires? I couldn't fit the pieces of the puzzle together.

As Mrs. Drucci said, "A policeman murdered him, but we sure gave him a grand funeral."

In answer to my request the rain came down harder than ever.

It is wrong to imagine, that in a familiar or playful correspondence, or letters of intelligence, the slip-shod muse is to be paramount. False grammar, in good society, is not tolerated, even en famille, *neither can it be in a letter.*

— THE NEW UNIVERSAL LETTER-WRITER,
Philadelphia, 1844

13

VINCENT BOGUNIECKI, the wiper ($85 a month), fugitive from an Illinois River town draft board, wiped the grease off his hands on his pants and again calculated the days left until his vacation time. The Second Mate came into the engine room all dripping, and handed him a letter wet with rain. Vincent leaned against the starboard engine and tore it open.

[125]

Vincent Boguniecki
Engine Dept.
Boat Inland Coal
Keokuk Lock, Iowa

August 12, 1942
PERU, ILL.

DEAR VINCE.

How are you feeling now? Better, I hope, because I'm not, I feel terrible I have been sick about all week. Rose and I went on the boat excursion last night & I was having fun and feeling fine until I got home. I had just gotten home and in bed when my nose started bleeding and did it bleed, wow! I just laid down and it started bleeding and the blood just poured for quite awhile. Mother got up and tried everything she knew and finally it stopped and almost too quick because it clotted in my head. But I finally got to go to bed but I was so weak by then that I was sick again all night. Well, I guess what we thought is true, I haven't seen a doctor yet I'm afraid to. I wish you would get a job in some defense plant like at Seneca, so I could see you instead of you off on those nasty boats. I get so lonesome and now this to worry about, Vince we ought to get married. Well Vince I don't know much else to write except I'm writing this in bed, I'm not working now, mother is making me stay home. They just announced over the radio that the boys who registered today they would take the ones from 18 to 20 not including the 20 yr. old boys, into defense plants for war work, they would take the 20 year olds for active duty but the others were too young. Goody. I am getting tired and another headache coming on so good bye for now.

Bye Now Darling
Love
VIVIAN

P.S. I Love You   x o x o x o x o x o x o

Joe came into the cheerful brightness of the galley, poked amongst the supper leftovers on the warming rack above the range, selected a brittle pork chop and a piece of slab cake with thin smeary icing on it, poured himself a cup of coffee from the Drip-O-lator, and stepping into the messroom sat down and slit open his letter with a table knife:

Mr. Joseph Denckman
c/o *Inland Coal*
U.S. Govt Lock
Keokuk, Iowa

HOTEL REGAL
ST. PAUL, MINN.
Aug. 8th

HELLO SWEETS.
Well. How goes it OK? See. I stick to my promise and am writing you like I said. I really felt mean about not taking you home with me but I have a rotten land lord. I'll see you when you get back and sure be waiting for you. I'll meet you at the "Troc" and from there we will go to this hotel. I meant everything I said so don't disappoint me — I'll say so long for the present, get rested up for honey, when we get together we certainly won't sleep OK? See you when you get here and call me soon as you get in and I'll meet you.
All my love.
SELMA BJONERUD

Joe speculated. She must be that one I picked up at the Brass Rail last trip. Now where did she get my address at?
Diamond was looking down at the puddles of rain in the coal on the deck and thinking of that ad on page 28 in the

[127]

Poultry Guide: "Just imagine a New Hamp Chicken but with white feathers and that lays WHITE EGGS instead of brown. Picture this chicken as having the WHITE EGG LAYING HABIT of fine White Leghorns, the HEALTH AND FORAGING QUALITIES of White Giants, and the DELICIOUS MEAT TYPE of Rocks or Reds. A true HEAVY BREED THAT LAYS WHITE EGGS is just what all of us chicken raisers want. Isn't it? HOW TO GET A START THIS YEAR!"

Not this year, Diamond was thinking, but maybe year after next — and just then Joe came along the lock wall above him and said, "Here's a letter, Diamond." Joe stuck the letter in his glove and threw it down. Diamond took the letter out and threw the glove back, and opened up the envelope and stood in the rain reading it:

Mr. Jas. Everhart
Towboat *Inland Coal*
C/o Lock
Keokuk, Iowa

Aug 11

DEAR JIMMY

Recieved your card and I am glad you are well and like your work. We are well and very busy house cleaning and working in the garden you should see our tomatoes. We had two of our chickens Sun for dinner & were they ever good we got 50 more last week. I called Lee Crewell & he said it would take a few weeks for the insurance co to get ready to settle but they will settle with you.

Had a letter from Bob and he is fine, Mary is still down there with him.

Margaret wrote and said Richie was fine and Earl is busy

with his garden too, and they are doing a lot of canning.

Well there isn't any more news so I will ring off. Take care of yourself & write.

Love, your sister,
GLADYS

"Now who is Bertrand Livingston Wainwright?" Joe said, standing in the doorway to the crew's lounge. "We got nobody with a name like that aboard I hope."

"Maybe that's that skinny little deckhand we picked up at Le Claire and he quit at Hannibal," one of the deckhands said.

"No, it ain't no skinny deckhand. That's what they just happen to named me," said the messboy.

"Well, here's a letter for you, Bertrand Livingston, honey," Joe said and went out.

The messboy went in the room he shared with the cook and got the cook to put down *Collier's* for a minute and the cook read the letter to him:

Mr. Bertrand Livingston Wainwright
Inland Barge Co. boat
Keokuk Lock, Iowa

Aug 12

DEAR SON,

Why don't you write? Got you questioners Sat from the draft board am sending them on. Do you get any vacation? We are not going to get any tiers we got papers to get 3 but we sent to Sears and they sent the papers back on account of some new law so Ralph and Ed are getting another ford off of Mush. Rettinges have a new baby boy. and you should hear our Bobie talk. Will close. Get one of the boys to write a leter for you.

MOTHER

[129]

Joe climbed up the iron steps at the back of the pilot-house, opened the door and went in.

"Cheer up, Cap, life ain't as bad as it seems — here's one of them pink envelopes. Then here's some others, and one from Chicago office."

"Thanks, Joe."

"Hell of a poor night out there, Jim."

"Hell of a poor night any night out on this god damn river," the Captain said, looking through the mail.

"Oh, my, you homesick again?"

"Ain't no place for a married man, Joe."

"Well, read that pink letter and you might feel better."

Joe opened the door and the rain drove in onto the linoleum. "On the other hand it might make you feel worse." He went back down to the deck, and Sargent, alone in the little glass house with the wind and rain pelting the panes, opened and read his mail:

Capt. Sargant
M/V *Inland Coal*
Keokuk Lock
Keokuk Iowa

BUENA VISTA IA
Aug. 6

CAP SARGANT DEAR SIR: —
I can not come back on the boat just now as my dad need me so bad in fishing after fishing is over if you want me I will gladly return and work for you I am as ever your Friend
HERBERT HINKLEY
P.O. Box 16, Buena Vista, Ia.

Well, that's a real good little deckhand, I'll have to keep him in mind when we go past there.

God, but Marie has the prettiest handwriting. I wonder how the baby is.

Captain James Sargent
M/V *Inland Coal*
U.S. Lock & Dam
Keokuk, Iowa

CENTRAL CITY, ILLS
Saturday night

DEAR JIM:

Got your letter all OK and glad you had a good trip and no trouble. Can't hardly wait for your vacation — you should see the baby, she is so good and eats so good, just like Ray used to. I got Ray a indian suit at Penneys and he just more than loves it — can't hardly get him to take it off for bed. They are getting worried about the corn — no rain here for nearly a month now and they are afraid the corn is ready to burn. The chickens look real good on that new mash and I will keep them on it even if it does cost more. That darn Si at the feed store never gets tired kidding me about it he calls it the Sargent Special mash. Ma is coming next week to help me with the canning, she claims she has not been feeling good again but Gert says it is just the usual talk, she will outlive us all. Well Jim I guess that's about it for now. I am always thinking of when you will come home for good and be with the kids. They just drive me crazy with Why doesn't Papa stay at home all the time like Uncle Jack and Uncle Bert. Well, I guess we can hold out until we get our nest egg — god knows you had a fight to get into some real money. Will close now.

Your loving wife   MARIE

P.S. Wetmore's setter has a litter of pups — of course Ray wants one.

He held the letter open and reached up and pulled off the overhead light, and he sat there in the dark listening to the rain drive against the panes and looking up at the lights of the lock and dam above the boat: "when you will come home for good and be with the kids."

He sat there for a long time thinking of home, of his boy Ray in his new Indian suit, of the baby in her crib, and Marie standing in the doorway of the bedroom, or combing her hair by the window.

After a while he turned on the light again and read the other two letters.

Master
Inland Coal
Keokuk Ia

HENNEPIN, ILL.

Master
Inland Coal
Received Suit case this A.M. but find several things missing.
A Green Plade Shirt, and a Red Plade Shirt, & Sweat Shirt.
Will be in St. Louis this Week End & will get in touch with you if you are there. Am Badly in need of the shirts so if I don't catch up with you please send it to 6027 Harpers Ave., St. Louis & check to same. Thank you for sending Suit Case & hope you can find them other clothes.

Yrs. truly,
BUD ELBING

Them deckhands must of gone through his suitcase before Al shipped it. What could he expect?

A STRETCH ON THE RIVER

INLAND BARGE COMPANY

BULK RIVER TRANSPORT

216 LA SALLE ST.
CHICAGO, ILL.
August 13

Capt. James Sargent
M/V INLAND COAL
U.S. Lock & Dam #19
Keokuk, Iowa

DEAR CAPT. SARGENT:

We have not received blue copies on orders as follows:

14683 coil line	15136 six red globes
14697 dozen pails	15137 six green globes
15101 six sets chain links	15149 marlin spike
15109 10 gals gray paint	15171 six cold shuts
15116 meat grinder parts	15183 two Patterson ratchets
15134 bale wiping rags	15197 searchlight carbons
15135 two kerosene lanterns	

Surely by this time you must have received at least some of the above items and we ask that you immediately check on this and sign and send us your blue copies.

Pay check for Hubert Crandall was sent to the MARCIA T. by mistake. Capt. Warren will forward to you at St. Paul.

Please send in barge damage report on IB112 which has cracked knuckle from collision with lockwall on Illinois river when in tow of the MONTGOMERY.

On arrival St. Paul check with Mr. Pearson regarding new Gorman & Rupp bilge pump.

Your clerk omitted to fill in beneficiary on insurance for mess boy Bertrand L. Wainwright.

On arrival Dairyland coal dock at Genoa, Wis., check with shore crew for two lashings left by the steamer ST. CROIX.

Yours truly,

G. E. WILSON
Assistant to Capt. Kelly

We finally got the tow hooked up and by the time we had the barges all tightened up and the lashings on we were out in the dark lake above the dam. I checked the running lights and turned the wicks up just a little bit and walked back to the boat in the rain. No, they wouldn't believe it, the boys back home, if I told them what I had been doing all evening. I went into the galley and got a cup of coffee and went into the messroom. My shoes were making a nice musical squushing sound.

"Keokuk lock," said Diamond. "Good-by, you bitch."

"That rain, man how it's acoming down," said Shorty.

"Here's a letter for you, Bill," Joe said. "Now I gotta go up and see what the mighty Sargent wants, if any." He went out, and I opened my letter and read it.

Lake Chad
Aug. 11, 1942

William Joyce
Inland Coal
Keokuk Lock
Keokuk, Ia.

WELL FIREBALL,

How you hitting it off with Horace Bixby and the boys? I presume you are wearing a white linen suit and smoking Wheeling stogies. Here the local pukes have got their hands

out of their pockets during the hot spell and are giving the
family interests a big play on gin preparations instead of the
usual beer; Papa is really taking it away from them, he says
business was never so good, even back with the Chicago connection in the old days. The slots are going night and day, he
has to spray them with ice water to cool them down once in a
while. You should have seen two leading young meteors of the
legal denomination over at the 66 the other night — they set up
stools in front of the quarter machines and had Chuck bringing them quarters so they would not have to descend and lose
time. Meanwhile their girl friends, two debutantes with eighth
grade diplomas in cutting up colored paper, named Charlene
and Thelma Mae, gorged on Tom Collins and exchanged mean
remarks about absent girl friends. Finally the judges gave up
trying to bust the western Illinois combine and after a final
round of insults at the girls they skidded out. Jeff Schwartz
came in with Cy and after criticizing the brandy confided in
everybody that Roosevelt is a Jew. Jeff doesn't look so good
any more, he is beginning to come unglued, but is still plen-
tifully supplied with fifty dollar bills, it's wonderful. Then of
course who trapped me but Fat Hohnecker and I had to listen
how Clarence had been awarded this medal for marksmanship
down at Fort Sill and Nick Kramer, who is home on leave and
has been lit for six days said: "Them marksmanship medals
are great. They give me one and I traded it for a package of
Trojans." Fat got sore and wanted to talk about it but Nick,
who plays the role of A Soldier Home On Leave in this drama,
decided this was the time to describe the benefits of army life
and it was not just the kind of a eulogy we usually hear over at
the Kiwanis Club. Finally Fat said, "Where is Bill at? Is he
in the service?" "No," I said. "He is hiding out in a cave near
Sherrills Mound living on roots and nuts." The point is that

Papa is about to cave in from the heat although he won't admit it and I think we should get him up to Duluth for awhile. Could you make it up there on your next leave or are you going to spend the whole time quimming in St. Paul? Let me know. We could do some fishing perhaps, or just sit and watch the swedes and the seagulls fighting it out for title to the iron range.

Yours for light wines and beer,

HERB

"Oh you silly bastard, Herb," I said laughing.

"Letter from home, huh?" Shorty said.

"Oh, that brother of mine, he's a comic, that boy," I said.

"I ain't spoke a word to my brother for nine years next month," Diamond said.

"How's all that come about?" Shorty said.

"We had a big fight. I hit him with a length of gas pipe. We ain't talked since."

"How old was you nine years ago, for the sweet Maria?"

"I was twelve years of age," Diamond said.

Joe came in from the deck, along with some of the rain.

"Here's a letter for you, Bill," he said. "I had it mixed up with the papers. I don't suppose it's nothing interesting though — it's wrote by a girl and is marked St. Paul."

"No," I says, "I suppose it's somebody that wants four dollars for the underprivileged Baptists in the polar regions."

"It could be from that there wonder girl, I suppose," Joe said. "The one in the motion picture business."

"Not a chance," I said. "She quit in the second grade. She can't write."

It was from Merle all right. I drank my coffee and just held the letter and turned it over and looked at it. What was inside might not be as thrilling as the feeling and appearance of the thing unopened.

"Why the hell don't you write me more regular if you're so daffy about me, then?" I asked her once.

"If I wrote you very much you'd find out how dumb I am," she said. "Anyway, you're not so interested in what I've got to *say*."

"Well, baby," I said, "lovers like us are supposed to write love letters, damn it."

"Kiss me some more," she said. "And take your shirt off for heaven's sake. Quit talking so much and keep your mind on your work. There, that's a little more like it."

After Shorty and Diamond had had enough to eat they wandered off up to the deck room. Joe was in the galley frying an egg and I was alone so I opened up Merle's letter and read it:

DEAREST BILL —
I've been thinking about you all day like you told me to when the wind is from the south. Not that it did me any good. It's been a hell of a long day and I feel like letting off steam. Why aren't you here instead of off someplace in Missouri — you're never around when I need you the most.

I know I tease you sometimes, but I don't really mean it, baby. Guess I'm just naturally mean, what do you think?

The new manager asked me to go out with him Sat. nite but I turned him down. Now he's P.O.'d at me I suppose.

A STRETCH ON THE RIVER

I should worry, I could walk right into the job over at the RKO Orpheum any time.

Tell that big handsome dutchman Joe that Irene got a new job she is in the office at Cudahy's. Likes it real well.

I wish to hell you would come and take care of your baby and quit chasing those St. Louis girls. You know there's something about you and me, lover, that is a little bit special. Come on up here, sweet stuff, and give me what we love.

All yours, and I mean *all*

MERLE

My stuff is for the gents. The squaws don't get me.

— THOMAS A. DORGAN

14

Out in the Dakotas all the babies had heat rash, and in South Chicago, Gary, Calumet, Hammond, and Blue Island the film fans were dragging themselves out of the air-conditioned dreamlands and back into the dreadful night. Back to the torrid bedrooms, back to the sticky bed sheets and the nocturnal buzzing fly, to revelations of future disappointments written on the ceiling. However, drink NEHI, WHISTLE, or CLEO COLA, suffering Christians, and in the morning things will seem better; remember, only three more days until Sunday when the bills change at all the theaters and then YOU'LL LAUGH YOU'LL ROAR AT THIS RIB-TICKLING MIRTH-PROVOKING FUN FESTIVAL IT'S A LAUGH RIOT FROM START TO FINISH. Laugh and the world laughs with you, cry and you get thrown out on your ear. Radio Papa, why is your aerial always down?

Despite the heat, which we, too, were feeling over on the Mississippi, I packed away two slabs of Swiss steak with gravy potatoes, some bullet peas, potato salad, peach preserves on bread, two dishes of jello and four or five store cookies with pink cream inside. Keokuk was behind us, there was plenty of free air available to all, and a cigarette tastes so much better when your muscles are all tight and hard from work, especially on the Upper Mississippi when the evening shadows commence to drop over the Iowa side, and the bluffs on the Illinois side are gold from the sunset.

Because in the beginning God made heaven and earth, and then He made steamboating. He collaborated with Shreve on the western river steamboat even before He turned His attention to girls.

And then He made girls, girls in their lovely fur coats and silk stockings or girls in their summer dresses, girls on Saturday night arm in arm on Main Street, girls in the fields in spring with their dresses around their ears, girls with dimpled knees on bicycles, girls leaning out of windows, washing their hair, or tickling themselves under the lilacs. Girls, god how I love them. Without them, cuckoo as most of them are, there is no point in anything, not even in work or steamboating or the river.

After supper we were sitting on the foredeck smoking and describing all the amazing events of our lives and all the women that had begged for our favors and Joe came up the deck from the galley wearing a clean uniform shirt and his visor cap.

"Hey Shorty," he said, "you and me and the Chief is going up to town. Bill, you and Diamond go back and toss the yawl in the river."

We dumped her in and Diamond and I gave Shorty some money to get us some ice cream. They got the outboard started and we turned them loose.

"You guys clean up the hole and splice them lines we parted," Joe hollered at us just as they took off.

"For just one small minute I thought he would forget about us," I said.

"No fear of that," Diamond said. "What's the town up ahead?"

"Muscatine," I said. "Let's get down in the hole and have it over with."

We took a good last look at the sentimental evening and plunged down into the forward hold. It was considerably hotter down there, about the right oven heat for orange coconut chiffon cake, and the smell of oakum and paint nearly flattened you. We cleaned up all the junk line and busted wires, and made piles of the lines that could be fixed. Then we sat down to splice, with the hatchet and a couple of blocks of wood. What with the jackknifing at the locks we parted quite a bit of line every trip, not so much our watch as the other watch, which had only one good deckhand and two greenhorns. Diamond and I did most of the splicing because we were the handiest at it; we didn't have any fancy stuff to do — just a short splice or an eye splice. The wires we spliced in the vise in.the engine room and we melted lead and poured deadeyes on the forward deck.

I took a lock line somebody had parted down at New Boston lock, and Diamond began with an old black lashing that must have commenced its career about the time the *Sultana* blew up with all the Union soldiers aboard.

"Lend me your jackknife," Diamond said, and I handed it over.

"When are you gonna get a knife of your own?" I said.

"I meant to get one in Alton this trip," he said.

"How could you get a knife when you lay in your bunk all afternoon?" I asked him.

"I was gonna give you the money for it," he said.

The messboy came down the ladder to get some potatoes. For some reason the locker was up here in the forward hold.

"What are you fellers doin?" says the messboy.

"I'm riding a bicycle," Diamond said. "And Bill here, he's playing the piano."

"Aw," says the messboy, "you're fixin them ropes."

"Pass over the hatchet," I said, and trimmed off the ends of my line.

"You fellers ain't suppose to smoke down here so the cook tole me," said the messboy.

"Aw fer chrissakes, get them spuds," Diamond said.

"Well, that's what he tole me, all the same," said the messboy, and he loaded up with cobblers and climbed the ladder.

"Now don't that guy beat hell?" I said.

"Oh well, can't expect too much offn him. He don't know no better."

"Pass me the hatchet."

"I wonder if Shorty will get that ice cream."

"He'll get it unless they run out of it up there."

"How big is this here Muscatine?"

"Oh — fifteen or twenty thousand."

"I wisht I was home tonight."

"I wish I was in St. Paul."

We got the hold pretty well cleaned up and went up for a breath of air. We climbed up the ladder and it was still light out. The Junior Engineer stuck his head out the engine room door looking for the wiper, and then went back to overhauling the old worn-out starboard generator. The wiper was standing around the corner having a smoke; he was all covered with oil and dirt.

"I wisht I could get a job in the engine room, don't you, Bill?" said Diamond.

"Yeh," I said. "So nice and cool and invigorating in there tonight. How about it, Vincent?"

"We got that god damn Fairbanks-Morse tore down agin," he said.

"Aw cheer up, Vincent," I said. "Maybe the Chief will let you ashore for half an hour when we get to St. Paul."

"Ain't that fine?" he said, and threw his cigarette in the river and went back into the engine room.

"Lend me your makins," I said.

"I hope Shorty brings that ice cream," Diamond said.

Night began to fall over the Upper Mississippi.

Sam Beard's nephew got three girls in trouble
one spring. The lawyer for the girls said to
Sam Beard's nephew's lawyer, "Where you
going to stand him next spring?"
OVERHEARD ON THE OHIO RIVER

15

WE RETREATED to the hold again, and left the
dew falling on the soft warm sand bars and the fishermen
in their skiffs going home with picnic baskets full of empty
beer bottles.

"What about this here Hitler?" Diamond said.

"No good," I said.

[145]

"That's the way I figure him. And them French and English, too. I wouldn't trust none of them. They . . ."

"Hey, wait a minute," I said. "They're on our side."

"I don't give a —— what side they're on. Take this here Duke of Windor, all he wanted to do was get to be King. He is so sore they won't let him be King he marries this here American girl and figures he'll be King of the U.S.A., by god, if he can't be King of England."

"But god damn it, man, he already *was* King. They bounced him out *because* he married Simpson."

"Sure, that's what they *say*. You wouldn't expect them to come right out and admit it, would you?"

"Admit what?"

"Why that he wants to kick out the Congress and run it like them old-time kings."

"But he hasn't even *been* to the U.S. yet, and they bounced him out over there four or five years ago already."

"How do you know he ain't been here yet? *They* never tell you nothing."

"But damn it, Diamond . . ."

"Listen, did you hear Cap toot for a deckhand?"

"No I didn't, did you?"

"Yeah, he blew twice."

"All right, I'll go see what the poor boy wants. Probably some coffee."

"Don't tell me nothing about them English. Them and the Russians and the Arabs and the French and the Argentines, they're all alike."

"All right, all *right*, let's forget about it," I said, and I climbed the ladder out of the hold.

It was dark outside now, and the glow of the town lay upstream on the port side, and the lights of the highway bridge were reflected in the river way up ahead. I figured the Captain wanted us to keep a lookout for the yawl. Or maybe he was worried about the Duke of "Windor" and wanted us to search the hold for bombs.

The radio was going in the pilothouse, and in the dark I located the Captain by the glow of his cigarette.

"Did you blow for a deckhand, Cap?" I said, closing the door.

"Those fellas in the yawl ain't back yet," he said. "You and Diamond stand by. There's the landing right over there."

"OK," I said, and turned to go.

"What you and Diamond been doing?" he said.

"We been in the hole splicing," I said.

"I wonder what happened to them damn fools," he said. He shot his cigarette out the forward window and it arched to the deck below. "I s'pose I better blow the whistle, but it won't do no good if they're in some dump with the juke box wide open."

He blew a landing whistle — two longs and three shorts — that echoed back from the grain elevator, and turned on his arc light and ran the beam up and down the landing.

"There's the yawl," I said, "but nobody around it."

"Damnation," he said. "Always something." And he reached forward and pulled the indicators to SLOW AHEAD. After a bit he stopped the engines and we drifted, our momentum dying, but still running upstream dead slow. No sign of anybody over on the bank.

Sargent blew another landing whistle.

"Wake up, sinners," he said. "Hear that whistle blow?"

On the radio some guy was getting off some jokes cribbed from *Brudder Gardner's Stump Speeches, Comic Lectures, and Negro Sermons,* A Galaxy of Amusing, Side-Splitting Oratorical Effusions (Muncie, Ind., 1898), and the studio audience was shrieking approval.

"Aw, shut your face," Sargent said, and he turned the radio off.

"This ain't like Joe and Curly at all," he said. "Now I wonder what went wrong. Say, Bill, get me a cup of coffee."

The cook had gone to bed and the galley was empty, with the stove turned low. The messboy was in the mess-room digging into *Batman Comics.* The coffee was none too good so I made some fresh. Diamond came into the galley.

"I wonder what happened to them guys," he said. "It ain't like Joe to miss the boat."

I took the coffee up to the pilothouse in a white mug, leaving some samples along the deck. Sargent blew a couple more times but there was no action over by the yawl.

"I hate to get ahead of those damn fools, with that out-board in the shape it's in, but I can't hold up the whole Inland Barge Line no longer," and he shoved the indicator to SLOW AHEAD. The wheels began to take hold and then he shoved her up to FULL AHEAD and pretty soon we commenced to crawl up against the current again.

I went out on the bridge on the port side of the pilothouse and leaned on the rail and kept a watch astern for the yawl. About the time we got through the highway bridge and above town into the dark again, I saw the light of an outboard overtaking us and I figured it must be them.

"Here they come," I said, going back through the pilothouse and heading for the deck.

Diamond was just coming out of the galley when I got there and the yawl was keeping alongside. The Captain turned on the deck lights and Joe brought the yawl in and I caught the line Shorty tossed to me. There was nobody in the boat but Joe and Shorty.

"Where the hell is Curly?" I said.

"He went to the church supper," Joe said.

I looked at Joe under the deck lights and he had a cut under his eye that was bleeding down his cheek. Then I looked at Shorty — he had a puffed-up eye and his red handkerchief was wrapped around his hand.

"I told you not to play around with those rough town girls," I said.

"Set the yawl on the roof," Joe said, and went in the galley and the screen door slammed behind him.

"Well, ain't you a happy god damn sight," Diamond said.

"Where's Curly?" I asked Shorty again.

"Last time I seen him he was between two cops."

"Lemme see your hand," I said.

"Well, I didn't get youse no ice cream," Shorty said.

After we got the yawl aboard we went into the galley. Joe had gone up to the pilothouse. We made a new pot of coffee and got into the lunch meat and rubbery cheese the cook had left out for us. Shorty unwrapped his hand

and it bled all over everything, including the bread knife and the mustard.

"Well, what happened?" I said.

"Yeh, where's Curly at?" Diamond said.

"Hold yer horses till I eat somethin," Shorty said, sticking a couple of pieces of ham sausage in some bread, "and I'll tell you about it. Ain't we got no pie tonight?"

"No, no pie," I said.

"Never mind the pie," Diamond said.

"Well, we went uptown," Shorty said, "and we went in this here saloon for a beer. Joe had a boilermaker, Curly had gin and Seven-Up, and I had a bottle Bud. So then we had a couple more and Curly took a few numbers on the punch board but he never hit nothin. Joe put some nickels in the juke box and I got me some of them potata chips and we were havin a real good time. The bartender was a pretty good guy about thirty-five and him and Curly got to chewin it over about the Ohio River — seems he was over in Cincinnati once and to hear him tell it the whole Ohio River quit business when he left. Then a couple girls come in with two ole boys but they didn't like it and went away. So Joe took a few punches at the punch board but he never hit. The prize was a cigarette case made to look like a automatic pistol. Real pretty with like pearl handles and all. Then a fella come in and set on the next stool to me and we got talkin. Seems he was farmin back here in the hills someplace so we had a good talk and some more beers. He had bad luck with hog cholery and to tell the truth I felt sorry for the poor bastard. My Uncle

[150]

Jim lost nineteen hogs last summer with the cholery."

"Listen," says Diamond, "you didn't get that eye from hog cholery, did you?"

"No," says Shorty. "Well, he went on home after a while, said he had to pick up his ole lady by some friends of hers. Joe struck up with a dude at the end of the bar with a white shirt on, and Curly was always talkin to this bartender. They was playin pool in the back so after a while I took my bottle of Bud and went back to the center table and got a cue, a damn poor cue too, but there wasn't no good cues to be had that I could find. The boy racked up and I shot myself a little practice game and went up and got another bottle of Bud — my, it was hot in there in spite of the fans.

"OK, pretty soon Joe come back and got a cue and him and me played a game. I beat. Then we played again and Curly come back and watched us with another gin and Seven-Up. Sure don't see how he can drink that stuff.

"About this time in come three soldiers. They took the next table and they were all pissed up and you know how them soldiers are. I shoulda knowed better but I figured aw hell we'll be draggin out soon anyways. One of these guys was a big son of a bitch about the size of Hank that ole deckhand we had on here, and about twicet as ignorant. The other two was just ordinary soldiers like you see every-place except from the way they handled their cues you could see they wasn't in a pool hall for the first time. Gimme the mustard.

"Well this big bastard started in with a big loud mouth

[151]

but we didn't pay him no attention but played our game.
I don't know how it started but he got to makin cracks
about us, and particularly about Joe every time Joe would
shoot. Like he was talkin about somebody else, but meanin
Joe. I seen Joe's pressure gauge commencin to raise and I
figured we better blow. But no, Joe wanted another game.

"About now Joe was makin a corner shot and the big
guy walks past between the tables and bumped Joe's cue.

" 'Beg yer pardon, junior,' he says.

" 'What?' says Joe, turnin around and this guy is about a
head taller.

" 'Go on, play yer shot, 4–F,' says the big guy.

"Did you ever see Joe in one of these here deals? Oh-oh,
talk about a punch! Ole Joe hauls off and throws one at
this boy and it sounded like somebody threw a pool
ball again the wall. The ole boy falls back on the table
and Joe hits him again and his nose starts to bleed. One
of the pals goes for Joe but Curly tosses his glass and all
on the table and spins him around and pastes him a good
one on the mush. The big guy is back in the game now and
lands one on Joe that woulda killed me, but Joe picks himself off the wall and he is mad now and he pokes that
bastard in the mouth and you can hear the teeth crackin.
The other soldier and I get into it and he gives me some
good ones and I landed one he ain't likely to ferget tonight
neither. Then the whole god damn joint went nuts, some
soldiers at the bar come into it, and the guys at the other
tables, crissakes I never seen such a mess, one ole boy begun
heavin pool balls and another one was swingin a cue, and

[152]

over went the juke box, and empty bottles was flyin around. Me and this here soldier was punchin each other when I got a bottle on the back of the neck. I got mad and turned around to see where it come from. Right then I got slugged in the eye. I hit him back and give it all I had and just then somebody conked the son of a bitch over the head with a cue. He opens his mouth and says Ow just as I hit him and his teeth like to cut my hand off. Joe was kickin it out of that big soldier by now, believe it or not — oh, man, what a sight. Somebody hollers 'The Cops,' and I run out the back way into the alley. I waited in the dark up the alley a ways and some of the boys come out and made tracks down the side streets. Pretty soon along come Joe. 'Where's Curly at?' I says. 'The cops got him,' Joe says. 'How'd you make out with the big boy?' I says. 'He's layin under the pool table,' he says. 'I give him a kick in the head as I was leavin that like to broke my ankle. I hope he enjoyed it. I reckon he'll know he was hit when he comes to.' We went around the side street and walked up the street acrost from the tavern and the cops were bringin the guys out. There's Curly between two cops, with his visor cap still on. They put him in a Chevvy squad car together with some of the others and off they go. Joe and me stopped in a little tavern and had a couple shots and waited around on Curly but he never showed up so we come back to the boat. I s'pose he's either in jail or he'll be up here at the lock. I don't blame Joe none. I had about enough of these here soldiers myself."

"I wish to hell I had seen it," I said.

[153]

"I don't miss it none," said Diamond.

"Ole Joe he throws a awful punch," Shorty said, dripping some more blood on the loaf of bread from his bashed-up hand.

"That would have done my heart good," I said.

. . . it must be said, however, that there was something providential in the zeal of the good missionaries in christening, as they did, the ports at either end of the upper river run. The mention of St. Louis and St. Paul lent the only devotional tinge to steamboat conversation in the fifties.

— GEORGE BYRON MERRICK

16

"DUBUQUE," Joe said. "What ever happened there, I wonder, besides morning, evening, and the middle of the day."

We were up above Dubuque in the pool north of Lock 11. A hell of a pool. Even the best pilots will tell you they don't like a bit of it. We were through what used to be

Maquoketa Chute and coming up on Parsons Bar Light and ready for the big bend where the river heads almost straight west, past Spechts Ferry and on up the line to North Buena Vista.

"You really want to know?" I said.

"Not much," Joe said.

"Then I'll tell you. First they opened the lead mines, and the Indians worked the mines until old Julien Dubuque put on a time study man and the Indians got sore and started the Blackhawk War. Meantime there was a rumor back East that the Elks' Club was starting up a new branch out West with eight pool tables and the bar whiskey ten cents a glass. This was the beginning of the westward movement."

"The last time I was uptown there," Joe said, "I run hard aground in that bar acrost from the hotel. 'Do you wanna go upstairs, honey?' says this little bitty black-haired grinder. 'I might as well,' I says, 'I been here an hour and no celebrities come in yet.'"

"Wait a minute," I said. "I only got up to the Louisiana Purchase. About this time Julien Dubuque got into an argument with his beautiful Indian wife Peosta over him setting around the house in an old cotton-flannel bathrobe all day without a shave listening to the baseball games, and the result was a decision in Peosta's favor after she beaned him with some book ends which one of the salesmen had given them for a wedding present. Julie got sore and went to visit his brother-in-law in Waukegan and won thirty dollars playing euchre."

[156]

"One time I was up there in that Coney Island acrost from the Western Union," Joe said, "and I clamped down on a hot dog and broke a piece right off my tooth. Look here. See that there piece gone? 'Well,' I says, 'that's the end. Life has turned out to be merely a hollow mockery.' 'What's that?' says the waitress, a farm type. 'I come in here broke,' I says. 'I got no job. I'm three hunnerd miles from home and look at the rain come down out there in the street. Now somebody left a piece of gravel in the chili sauce and I just busted my side tooth off.' 'Well,' she says, 'you won't have to pay for it then. But listen,' she says. 'You can't go out in that rain.'"

"Say, does this story have a happy ending?" I said. "Now that you interrupted and ruined my history of old-time Dubuque, I'd like to hear something cheerful."

The Milwaukee two-car gas train came ambling down under the bluff and around the bend. The conductor gave us a wave from the rear vestibule. Over in the shade by the tracks a lady in a sunbonnet was fishing out of a skiff.

"'I got noplace else to go *but* into that rain,' I says. 'I come in with two bits for refreshment and shelter,' I says, 'and I go out into the rain broke and with a busted tooth. That's life,' I says. 'There's the whole blame story in a peanut shell.'"

I was looking upriver — you are always looking upriver or down river, at the channel, or the sky, or to see if there's a steamboat coming — but I was thinking of Joe in that Coney Island. It was steamy and warm in there, and the candy bars were tilted row on row beside the cash register.

The rain was sliding down the plate-glass window and through it, distorted by the rain, you could see the cars and the buses moving slowly in the street.

"Playing this scene kinda heavy, weren't you?" I said.

"Whadda you mean, heavy?"

"Well, how about 'Life has turned out to be merely a hollow mockery'?"

"Hell, I got that out of a story in *Argosy* magazine."

"And 'I came in for refreshment and shelter'?"

"Listen, Shakespeare, what makes you think you got a monopoly? I thought that up by myself. Any law against that?"

"Not yet," I said. "Then what happened?"

" 'Listen,' she says again, 'you can't go out into that rain.' 'Why not?' I says. 'I spent most of my life in the rain so far.' Poetic stuff, ain't it? And she went over and took her pencil out from her back hair and wrote something on a paper napkin. She gave it to me: '476½ Nebraska Street,' it said. 'Go on up,' she says. 'I'll be along in an hour. You can't stay out in that rain,' she says."

"This is right out of *True Story*," I said. "Fill it out. How was she?"

"She wasn't. I never seen her again. I put the piece of paper in my pocket and hit the rain. Never went ten paces and ran smack into Dude Beckwith off the *T. B. Collier*. 'Joe,' says Dude, 'I'm uptown lookin for a deckhand. What you doin here in the rain?' 'Lookin for a deckhand's job,' I says. 'Come on,' he says. 'Let's get a cab and go up to Eagle Point and catch her.' 'We'll be a long time on the boat, Dude,' I says. 'Well, just one,' says Dude, and we went into that dump acrost from the theater and had two drinks at company expense."

If it had been me I'd have told Dude I was taking away from a saw up at the sash and door factory, and gone up to the girl's place. But Joe wasn't so interested in the unforeseen promises of life as I am.

"You silly bastard," I said. "Me, I would have told him I was on the bank and gone on up to Nebraska Street."

"Sure you would have," Joe said. "But I didn't. I'd rather ride the *T. B. Collier* any day than some old girl from out in the alfalfa."

"What happened on the *Collier?*" I said, wondering if I would have taken the job.

"Old man Van Patten was on her as roof captain in them days and the pay was forty-two dollars a month. We didn't work a square watch. It was catch as catch can. And we was hung up most of the time. I carried line and rigging till the hide on my shoulders was like hamburger. But them was the good old days we hear so much about, and we never set up a roar about working conditions or put in a complaint because they was too much pressed meat for the nine o'clock lunch."

I've been ashore in Dubuque. It's strictly Upper Mississippi. A lot of high-pressure pilots and mates that started life under the thirty-dollar-a-month regime come from there. And they've got a cable railway to the top of the bluffs. From up there in the fall of the year the East Dubuque hills are all red with the sumac. That is, in the daytime. In the night East Dubuque is just a big neon splash with saloons side by side down each side of the only

street. You can buy grain alcohol in pints, or imitation black-
berry-flavored pear wine, or you can get in the back room
and shoot craps. The drunks lie groaning in the alleys while
the floor show goes on and on, forever and ever: grinning
tap dancers, sister acts, singers that put on wigs, emcees
that embarrass, and even dogs.

"No," Joe says, "I never went up to that girl's room, but
I always wondered what would have come out of it if I had.
She wasn't no tramp. She looked like she could milk, make
bread, and sing alto in the choir. Her complexion was like
springtime in the back country, and when she give me her
address she didn't have nothing bad in her mind. There's a
few girls left in the country like that."

"There's a few Frenchmen around that don't talk French,
too," I says. "But they're in the minority."

"You talk pretty," Joe says. "But sometimes you talk too
god damn much. You must of had some bad times to take
such a rough attitude toward the girls."

"I been hit pretty hard in my time, kid," I says. "But
if this girl struck you so good, how come you followed
Beckwith up to the boat so fast?"

"I'll tell you, Bill. I come down to the river from the
farm one time with a load for the grain elevator. I seen a
steamboat going past town, with the smoke pouring from
her stacks and the wheel tossing up a big white waterfall,
and I was through on the farm. Since then I been steamboat crazy. I couldn't do justice to no girl with the steamboat fever in my blood. Whenever I meet a girl I'd like to
settle down with I think of the long days away from her

[160]

on the boat. I'd rather keep out of it and stay happy. I got plenty of girls, all the way from Cairo to the Falls of St. Anthony, but I never yet sat on a timberhead here in the evening wishing to god I was back home in some two-room flat."

"Dubuque's right in the middle of the run," I said. "You could get off going upstream every trip with the right captain."

"I don't wanna get off every trip coming upstream. That would make it even worse."

"You disappoint me," I said. "Well, thank god the Good Lord created all different kinds of people."

"Well," Joe said, "I'll go up and set around the pilothouse awhile and soak up some knowledge. You hunt up Diamond and make up a new lock line and clean up the hole."

"Yes sir, boss man," I said. "You know, I think I'll get in my time and go for Mate's License. I'd like to hear what Captain James Sargent has to say when he is on his throne in the pilothouse." I had an idea that up in the pilothouse they talked about the channel all the time, or told stories like Sam Clemens.

Joe went up to the pilothouse to listen to the old-time steamboat talk and I went to look for Diamond.

A few minutes later, the messboy came down in the hold where we were busy splicing.

"I was just up in that little room on top and the Mate he tole me to tell you to get a bucket of suds and come up and scrub the floor."

"What little room on top? What you talking about, boy?"

"Why that there little room on top of the boat with all the glass windows."

"Oh, the parlor, you mean," says Diamond.

"Anyways, you're asposed to go up and scrub the floor."

"How you know he meant me?" I said.

"Well, he says the deckhand with the mustache. That's you, ain't it?"

"Yeah, that's me," I said.

"My cousin Andy he got a mustache."

"That's great," I said. "What's he do with it?"

"Do with it? He don't do nothing with it. He just leaves it set there."

So I got a bucket of suds and some rags and the scrub brush and climbed up to the pilot house.

Joe was sitting in one of the wicker chairs smoking. Sargent was at the steering levers and Curly, the Chief Engineer, was leaning out the forward window on his elbows looking up the river. We were going up through Rosebrook Crossing. I got down on my knees and began to scrub the floor.

"No, my old lady put up with that washing machine for six months and then traded it in on a Maytag," the Chief said. "She likes the Maytag fine."

"What soap does she use?" the Captain asked.

"Well, she started out on Beach's Pride, but later she went over to Rinso. Now she don't use nothing but Rinso."

"My wife she won't have Rinso in the house," the Captain said. "She's sold on Duz. She claims she can't do nothing with the sheets on Rinso."

"I don't know about that. My wife claims she never got such white washes before. What kinda machine you got?"

"A Regal Automatic."

"Well, no wonder. Them Regals is no good. They're nice and handy and all, but damn it they just don't clean the clothes. My next door neighbor down home, he's the druggist, he got one. Don't tell me about no Regal. What kinda vacuum cleaner you got?"

"Hamilton-Beach."

"How you like it? They claim that's a fine machine."

"They claim right. When it comes to vacuum cleaners the Hamilton-Beach gets right down to work and does the job. We had a Cyclone when we was first married, then we traded on a Kleen-Rite. When we finally broke down and got a Hamilton-Beach my wife says, 'Now we got a vacuum cleaner.'" He shoved his chair back and stood up. "Wouldn't you think them gover'ment engineers would dredge by mistake someplace just once where we need it? By god there's enough sand in this crossing for the Sahara Desert."

"Well," says the Chief, "I spent good money for a Revelation, and the damn thing won't hardly pick up a cigar ash offn the rug. My wife she says, 'Listen, honey,' she says, 'the Revelation people may call this a vacuum cleaner,' she says, 'but I don't.'"

"Oh," says Captain Sargent, "I already heard about them. My brother-in-law right down here in Dubuque, he runs the Elite Café, he got stuck with one of them. 'That

god damn thing,' he says. 'Why the gover'ment ought to
step in and close them people down. That ain't no vacuum
cleaner. That's a joke, that's what it is.' "

"He's about right. Mine ain't no good. How's his restaurant business?"

"He cleared about 3800 last year. But he has hell getting
help. He's got one waitress coming and one on her way
out all the time. He wants to get out and get himself a
grocery store."

"Grocery store! You better tell him to stay where he's
at. There ain't no money in a grocery store. Only trouble
and long hours. Why man, I was practically raised in a
grocery store. My old man went bust three times with
groceries."

"That's what I tell him, but he's set on a grocery store.
He's a buck, that boy. He's gotta find out everything the
hard way. Nobody can tell him nothing."

"He sounds about on the order of my sister's brother-in-
law down at Golconda. He got the idea he was gonna get
rich running these here 16-millimeter movie shows in the
country towns. 'They ain't no money in it, Vergil,' I told
him. 'You better stay on at the feed store,' I says. 'You
ain't gonna get rich runnin movies over at Carrsville or
Tolu. If you take my advice,' I says, 'forget about the 16-
millimeter picture shows and go up to Louisville and get in
one of them distilleries, Vergil. I can get you a job in any
of them through Cousin Ralph.' So naturally he got himself a movie outfit, and he had his first show out someplace
on the road to Eddyville with sixteen kids, seventeen dogs,
and the village whore for an audience. It went on like

[164]

that for a while but he was such a buck he wouldn't give in. Finally all his money was gone and the company come and took the machine away from him."

"What's he doing now?" the Captain asked, as he reached up for the whistle cord and blew two short toots for a deckhand to come up to the pilothouse.

"Back at the feed store. He's saving up now to take a mail course in Diesels. He raises chinchillas on the side. The only reason he took up chinchillas was because his cousin Bud told him there was no money in it."

"Joe, what you got the watch doing?" the Captain said.

"They're down in the hole making up a new lock line and cleaning up," Joe said.

"That other watch goes through lock lines as fast as we can make them up, it seems. The office is gonna start asking questions pretty soon."

"If Al would let that deckhand off the Federals stand the head line maybe they wouldn't part so much line," the Chief said. "He's got that little kid from Hannibal on the head. No wonder. That kid's about as useful as my grandmother out on the tow."

"I guess Al knows what he's doing," Sargent said. "Anyway that kid ain't dropped no buckets of paint yet." That was a slam at one of the wipers, a dumbbell from Rock Island who dropped a gallon can of inside white on top of the starboard generator.

Shorty opened the door and came in.

"Think you'll ever amount to anything, Shorty?" the Captain said.

"I doubt it, Cap," Shorty said.

"Seeing as how we're all working so hard up here how about bringing up three coffees?"

"You bet, Cap. Want some pie or a samwidge or sumpthing?"

"I guess I could use a piece of pie," the Captain said. "But none for Joe. His girlish figure is getting all outa shape."

Shorty went out and down the iron stairs.

"There's a good deckhand," Sargent said.

"Yeah," Joe said. "Shorty's a deckhand all right."

"The first thing I gotta do when I get home," the Chief said, "is to hang wallpaper in the upstairs hall." He lit a large cigar.

"I don't envy you none," Joe said.

Year after year while the stars above in the blanket of blue twinkle in Morse code, this rough he-man talk about soap powder goes on, while the ghost of Joseph Conrad, huddled behind the water cooler, listens in horror and surprise. Marlow, pass that bottle!

"When I get home I got to put up more shelves in the fruit cellar . . ." the Captain said.

Always twist the lids on tight on them jars when you throw 'em overboard. Somebody down river kin use 'em.

— THE COOK

17

THIS was the night Shorty got drowned. A hot evening that started off as a failure right from the time the messboy came into the pigpen and called us at 5:30. I came to life reluctantly, tangled in my sweat-soaked sheets, and immediately was clunked with a ferocious headache. Shorty was sitting on the edge of his bunk staring at his gruesome vegetable toes.

"A way to live, ain't it, Shorty?" I said, squeezing my head between my hands.

"But that's the way we like it," he said, and began to pull on his rockford sox.

I took three aspirins with some warm water labeled UNFIT FOR DRINKING, went aft and sat down at the mess table. Cook had set out two platters of corned beef and cabbage, and the butter plate had overflowed onto the tablecloth. I ate some canned peaches. A fly was doing the Australian crawl in the butter. The messboy swabbed his face with the dish towel.

The Chief came in and took a look at the supper, wiped off his glasses and said, "I s'pose when we get them snappy days next winter and the deckhands is chopping the lines off the deck with axes we'll have fruit salad and ice cream for supper. Where's the chili con carne — ain't you got none, Harry?" He went out and stood in the shade on the starboard side drinking his coffee.

I got my gloves and cap and hunted up the watch. This heat wave had been dragging on much too long — we were getting sick of it.

The watch was on the port side of the boiler deck doing the painting we should have done in April. The sun glared on the fresh, sticky white paint and blue flies arrived and departed, inspired to frenzied buzzings by the fumes of turpentine. I relieved Frankie and he went to eat while I took up where he had left off on the painting.

Shorty, unaware that his Maker had the finger on him for tonight's performance, and that before the watches changed again he would be down there lying waterlogged on the soft muddy river bottom with the friendly catfish nibbling his shoelaces and going through his pockets for jujubes, came down the deck, relieved Mush, and began to paint.

We were up in some pretty good country now. On our port side we were passing Capoli Bluff, and Chafalaya Bluff and Lansing, Iowa, were just up ahead. On the starboard side there were a bunch of little islands and grassy clumps, sloughs and backwashes, with the redwings playing tag among the willows and the kingfishers swooping down from the elm trees. We were 450 miles above Alton and that afternoon with Toots and Darlene was getting farther and farther away. Upstream 180 miles was the Smith Ave. Bridge at St. Paul, so it was about time to start getting in a sweat about Merle. Which watch would make the landing? Would we get there at night or in the daytime? What if we didn't wait for the empties but came right on down without a layover? What if she had a date? What if she was out of town? Where should I take her? What tie should I wear? Suppose there was a taxicab strike. Should I call her from Hastings lock? Did I need a haircut? Take her a box of candy? Act debonair or appealingly sad? How about flowers? How about bed? In introducing her to a casual acquaintance, a good friend, and a Methodist preacher, whose name should I mention first? Would I make these common grammatical errors: *I ain't, he seen, we done, they hadn't ought to of went?*

Joe came down the deck.

"Knock off, boys," he said. "Even the carp and buffalo are taking it easy tonight."

[169]

A buffalo is a fish uglier than a carp. A carp is a fish uglier than anything but a buffalo. A catfish is a collar ad compared to either.

"Clean up the brushes and do your routine stuff and then keep out of sight. And for chrissake close the paint up *tight.*"

"Hey, Joe," Shorty said.

"What?"

"Where's the next lock?"

"Genoa. We should be up there about eleven o'clock. Just in time to give you some exercise so you can sleep good."

"That's what I need, exercise," Shorty said.

"Look up there," I said, pointing up in the sky. A hawk was wheeling above the top of the bluff.

"I seen a eagle up above Lynxville last trip," Shorty said.

"Kinda pretty, ain't it, the way he floats up there," Joe said.

"Look a lot prettier nailed to the side of the barn," Shorty said.

"You god damn farmer you, Shorty," Joe said.

We cleaned up the brushes and put the paint away, swept off the foredeck, coiled down the lines, sounded the barge that was leaking, checked all the couplings, carried out a new lock line to the head, threw coal at a floating varnish can, trimmed and lit the running lights and carried them out to the head of the tow, and finally sat down by the engine room door; we sat on the deck with our backs against the steel bulkhead, smoked cigarettes and considered the approach of evening in the river valley.

A STRETCH ON THE RIVER

This is old Indian country up in here; we were right below where they fought the battle of Bad Axe in the Blackhawk War. It wasn't much of a battle — the Indians were starving to death and the U.S. Army knocked them off like target practice. The faces of the high bluffs are sharp limestone cliffs that come straight down to the river, and where there is a break in the bluffs, the green hills that run down into the valleys between are in pasture, with birch trees and red cedars on their steep slopes. In the early morning the mists hang down in these valleys, and in the evening the steamboat whistles echo on the golden bluffs just the way they did a hundred years ago when the *Grey Eagle* and the *Key City* and the other packets were up in here bringing civilization, sour-mash whiskey, and the profit motive to the upper valley.

"Seven years on the river and all I got to show for it is a paper suitcase full of dirty shirts," Shorty said.

"What do you do with all your money?" I said.

"Send some to my ma and piss away the rest."

From the islands came the cries of the pterodactyls, and the ghosts of Indians and raftsmen wrestled amongst the bats, bugs and fireflies under the trees. And dead fishermen, dead Sauks and Foxes and Winnebagoes, dead deckhands, Sunday swimmers, half-breeds, priests, marine engineers, and mates long dead came out of the river mud and rapped on the bottoms of the barges.

"Shorty, why don't you go back to the farm?"

"I ain't never gonna quit the river."

"Your uncle will give you that farm when he dies."

"I doubt I ever leave the river."

Yes, we were alone here. No clubs to join, no rich to envy, no taxis to dodge. Pretty scenery and plenty of coffee with Pet milk. No light bill, no gas bill, no telephone ringing all the time. The music of the Diesel engines, and our own wit to admire.

"I fell in the Ohio River four times on one trip when I was on the *Transporter*," Shorty said. "We was running from Helena, Arkansas, to Cincinnati."

"They got a streetcar there in Cincinnati that goes up the hill on a cable railway," I said.

"I never was uptown in Cincinnati."

"They call it the incline."

The cook came up the deck, fondling his cigar. "You guys din't eat much," he said.

"I ain't about to eat much," Shorty said, "as long as it stays this hot. Especially corned beef I ain't."

"I suppose you would of liked some chicken salad and a glass of lager beer. I give it up!" the cook said, throwing his arms up in an Oliver Hardy gesture of hopeless resignation. "I can't please this crew! I better go back to Peoria. I ain't doing no good here."

"Harry, everybody's kinda jumpy from the heat," I said in a voice intended to be soothing.

"I threw ten dollars' worth of corned beef in the river tonight," he said, and plopped off down the deck, colliding with the Junior Engineer who was just emerging from the engine room to see if the world was still outside.

It is no sin to be dead and it might be a pleasure, so why cry over Shorty, he had no tiny tots who would end up at the county home. He was the only one aboard who read the Bible and was therefore convinced of a heavenly home, and by the time he found out the story had been a little exaggerated he wouldn't know the difference anyway. We would miss him for a few locks and then we would get a deckhand to take his place and divide up his clothes among us and send his suitcase home with our worn-out clothes in it and after that we would just remember him once in a while.

We had passed Lansing, where the Main Street runs right down the bank and into the river, had managed Lansing Bend, one of the more famous sharp bends, had passed Indian Camp Daymark and Indian Camp Light (Flashing White, 4 seconds, 2 flashes), had put Big Lake Light, and De Soto, Wis., behind us and were coming up on Lost Channel Lower Daymark. It was night now, and Shorty and I moved around to the foredeck to get a little breeze.

"What's that light up ahead, Bill?" Shorty said, sitting down on a pile of lashings.

"That's Lost Channel," I said.

"How far from the lock?"

"Well, then there's Victory Bend and State Line and Bad Axe Island and Bad Axe Bend and Bad Axe River and then Island 126 and then Genoa lock."

"Never mind the geography lesson. Are we gonna get that god damn lock on this watch?"

"Yes, sunshine, we are," I said.

The Junior Engineer came out of his hole and sat down on the double bitts.

"There ain't a pump on this here boat worth its weight for melting scrap," he said. "I never packed pumps and overhauled pumps like this before."

"I got to get me some new gloves when we get to St. Paul," Shorty said.

"Here we sit," I said, "and the whole world is going to smash."

"I wonder what that little blonde bum of mine over in Illinois is doing tonight," said the wiper, as he leaned against the capstan.

Above us we could occasionally hear muffled sounds from the pilothouse: Joe's voice, the radio roaring with static, Sargent whistling, the door closing. Once in a while Sargent would turn on one of his searchlights to pick up a channel buoy, and the blinding ray of arc light would shoot out over the long rows of coal piles and way up the river so you could see a mile, clear as day. The bats and bugs and Mormon flies whirled in the death ray like an illustration from *Weird Tales*.

"Bill," Shorty said, "let's you and me go out and check them runnin lights."

"All right," I said. "Maybe there's a little more breeze out there."

We stepped over the jockey wires and started off down between the barges. Shorty was ahead of me, crunching along in the grit on the decks, and he began to warble in that Beardstown voice: "Please do to me, what you did to Marie . . ."

We passed the first coupling. The water was boiling up between the barges and the wires were creaking.

[174]

"A bottle of Budweiser would go over big with me right now," I said.

We reached the second coupling.

" 'Work is worship, labor holy.' Did you know that, Shorty?" I said.

"She's rough and tough, boys," Shorty said, "but that's the way we like it."

At the third coupling we stopped and rolled cigarettes and looked back at the boat.

"Man, look at the stars out tonight," Shorty said.

We reached the head of the tow. Shorty tripped over the lock line, slipped in the loose coal on the deck and pitched over the head of the barge into the river.

"God love him, he'll never come out from under the barges alive," I thought, and I set up a shout and ran for the boat.

We got out the yawl and fished around but we never found him, of course. We lost so much time the other watch had to make Genoa lock, which was some consolation but not much.

Shorty came up about a week later — a fisherman towed him to shore and they shipped him back to Beardstown via C B & Q.

"Karamazov," cried Kolya, "can it be true what's taught us in religion, that we shall all rise again from the dead and shall live and see each other again, all, Ilusha too?"

— DOSTOEVSKI

18

"Now I went and done it," Shorty thought, "here I am about to drownd, how and the hell did I ever pull such a dumb one as that?"

Just then his head hit the steel bottom plates of the barge rake: *crack!* and the current shoved him around the bottom of the rake and under the barges.

"This is worse than the carnival," Shorty thought. "So long Ma, so long boys. It's hell to die so young," and he did so. He felt better immediately.

"It sure is one hell of a lot cooler now, and no more worryin about which watch will get Keokuk lock. Poor Bill, I bet he like to had a hem'rage when I went over. Now they have got the engines stopped, and Joe and Bill and Diamond are gettin the yawl out to look around for me, I must be clear back to the first coupling by now, or maybe by the boat, but I don't hear the generator, I don't hear nothin. They can have my stuff but I hope they send my watch belonged to Pa home. Sargent will go crazy — oh, how he hates a drowndin on his boat. And I had no lifejacket on after all his preachin — that will make him even wilder. No sleep for the Captain, I'll give him bad dreams for a week. Well, I'm down here to stay for a while and I know one thing sure, I will never get back to that lock. We must of been right at Victory Bend when I took that dive. I suppose if I can get around the bend without goin aground I will make her down past Lost Channel to De Soto. It all depends on how much water I am drawin by that time. If I would of ate more for supper I s'pose I would drift a little closer to the surface in a couple of days. If I can stay out of the weeds and them little sloughs and cricks down by Indian Camp, maybe I can make her around Lansing Bend about the time I am gettin ripe. If I could get picked up there it would be handy, a nice thing to pull on a guy out in a yawl with his girl, but if I get past Lansing where am I — down the crick and no paddle, nothin below there clean to Lynxville and I would get lost in the pool sure. Maybe some duck hunters next fall would ketch what's left of me by then; if I can flank in at Lansing somehow and kind of bob around in there by them fishermen's boats they will see me, more'n likely they will be lookin for me anyways. I suppose Cap will tell them at the lock and they will all know it from here to Guttenberg and be on the lookout for me. That is gonna be tough gettin past them bends and out of the sloughs without no Pilot's License. I will look nice in a box there on the baggage platform of the Milwaukee at Lansing. Poor Ma. Looks like I ain't ever gonna see Beardstown again or find out how Uncle Jim's corn come out. They all tole me I was crazy to go roamin off on the river when I could of worked on the farm. Funny the way I was standin there that day watchin the flood and along comes ole Batty Welch, but I didn't know him then, he says, 'Boy, how would you like to work on a steamboat?' I says, 'I never give it no thought.' Yes sir, that was the old *Western Belle*, a beat-up little coal burner with a split wheel. After the first time we come down the Chain of Rocks and past Burlington Elevator and on down under McKinley Bridge and then on down under Eads Bridge and I see the lights of St. Louis and the boats tied up, the Federal boats and the Streckfus boats and the old *Ralph Hicks* rotting away and the showboat and the *Golden Eagle* and the *Susie Hazard* and them big smokestacks up in the air across the river at Cahokia, after that I never could go it no longer down the corn rows. Never would be here now layin under the tow so far from home in the Upper Mississippi if I hadn't just a been there that day

[179]

Batty come along and he says, 'Boy, how would you like to work on a steamboat?' Was I ever green and they sent me to the Engineer to fetch a bucket of steam, but how the hell did I know the difference? And the first time we made a yawl play at Havana they made me watch the yawl while they went uptown and got beered up. I remember it was a hot afternoon and there was a dead carp layin on the bank where the water had gone down, and an old boy was tryin to patch up a motorboat and I talked to him. I bet Bill will be all tore up about this, the poor bastard will figure he coulda grabbed me, I be god damned if I can figure how come I fell off that barge — I knew that lock line was there, right where it always is, laid out in bights — seems like I slipped in that loose coal on the deck. I always thought it was a lot of bull sweepin them decks off but look at me now, boys, look at me now, no more beer and no more girls — I ain't never goin to see that ole Marth no more. It grieves me when I think back on that time we was makin hay to her dad's place and we went down to the crick in the evenin, nobody never caught on. We got all mosquito bites and then we use to get in the crick and do it under water. I wonder where Batty Welch is now, I heard he was pilot on the *Chicago Bridge,* and then again some deckhand off the *Hurley* told me he was a mate on one of the *City* boats, he took me in hand and he says, 'Boy, I'll make a deckhand out of you, and you'll be ridin these cinder throwin devils till you lay down someday and die out on the barges.' Well, I'm dead all right but I'm under the barges, not on 'em. Then when we broke up our tow there at Cottonwood Island we had barges all over the river and two down through the Burlington railroad bridge and one went down and hit the Quincy highway bridge — we was out there thirty hours and run through a couple of new coils of line and Jackie Winders fell overboard and come near to drowndin. When we was all done and had her made up and Captain Leverett had her goin up the river again we was settin there on the barges too tired to even go back to the galley for coffee, we was right abreast of Hogback Island and Batty says to me, and he give me a tailor made, he says, 'You done good, kid, you done good, you'll make a deckhand yet, even with the manure still in your shoes you're a better deckhand than some I know.' He meant that wise guy — what was his name, Ken something? — from St. Louis who was always ravin about all the big boats he been on, ole Batty couldn't stand the sight of him. I wonder if Marth is still workin there in the café. What will she think when she sees it in the paper: 'Randolph Calhoun drownded on the Upper Mississippi, an employee of the Inland Barge Line and the nephew of Jacob Randolph, route #2.' I must be clear of the boat now and them poor bastards are out in the yawl and Al is out of bed and the other deckhands they got them up to tie the tow off, I reckon, and Bill is givin his version of it again, the poor bastard. They got a fine chance of findin me tonight with no life vest on and the river dark anyways; if the *Sprague* was sunk in the middle of the channel they couldn't find her tonight, dark as it is. Then after the *Jane Collins* Batty took me over onto the Federal after he got a watchman's job over there. We spent the summer on the *James W. Good* until I fell in that empty

[181]

lease barge one night at Red Wing and was laid up — it
was nice in the hospital and they give me magazines to
read. The next season I went back on the Illinois on the
Betty Jane but the less about that season the better. Then
I got on the Federals again for two seasons and worked for
Uncle Jim in the winter. And then there was the *Transporter* from Cincinnati to Helena and ole Cap Saunders
— he was all right except when he would get on the bottle
and Flea Williams and I would stand watch together. Flea
was a comical bastard — I can laugh myself sick now
thinkin of some of the rare ones he use to pull — then he
got married and went to work in a fillin station in Hannibal.
She's been a grand ole time and I'd just as soon be down
here makin friends with the catfish as of spent all my days
shovelin manure and plantin corn. I sure hope they fish me
outa here, though. I don't hanker to stay down here after
the heat wave is over. Ole Joe will be sore he got nobody to
help him with the jackknifin, I s'pose he will get Bill to
help him jackknife and leave Diamond handle the head
line and get one of the other watch to stand the stern line.
They will prob'ly pick up a deckhand up at La Crosse or
Winona or Fountain City if they can find one, some kid
out of a ice cream parlor that will last for about two locks,
maybe they can get one of them guys at Genoa on the way
down, some good deckhands around there. Well, he's got
ole Bill and Diamond anyways and they can hold up their
end any time. Here goes my chance at relief watchman I
been in line for — Al told me Sargent had me in mind for
relief man when he went on next vacation — ain't that the
roses though? Then let's see, after the *Transporter* I went

over on the dredge for a while and then on the *Mackenzie* on the Upper Mississippi and spent the summer foolin with that ole fuel flat and we hit the Burlington Bridge and took half the pier right on up the river with us; the ole *Mack* never even hesitated and the limestone blocks and half the bullnosing was right on the deck of the barge. After that I went over to the Illinois again on the *Marcia T.*, quite a comedown after the big *Mack*, and we messed with them ice cakes all winter and punched a hole in her bottom at Marseilles and all got off but the messboy — when they raised her they found the poor bastard down in the hole. Lookin for some soap powder, I suppose, when she went down. And we use to go over there to the Ace of Clubs by the landing in Joliet and play the juke box and get lit up and go out in a cab to them whorehouses when we got a chance, and then two months on the little *Mortimer Jones* in the drainage canal and a few trips down the Sag to South Chicago with one load at a time but that run gets old awful quick and I asked for transfer and got onto the new boat and we run from Joliet to Havana and every time you looked up there was some more out of the Chicago office comin aboard with their wives to see the new boat and the port captain was around all the time and Captain Ferris had to show them what a big rough tough ole boy he was and had the megaphone stuck out the pilothouse all the time. What a joke — not only that but all them landins every other day and makin up eight loads at a time, carry out all that riggin just to carry it back forty hours later and make up all over again. To make a long story short, then I tole them I had enough of it and

[183]

they transferred me to the ole *Inland Coal* and yours truly
is now under water for good. I don't see I can make it
down to Lansing. Thank god they's plenty of fishermen
around here, maybe one of them will pick me up. She's
a rough go and that will be tough gettin past them bends
and sloughs without no Pilot's License."

And then Shorty was clear of the barges and the towboat, but instead of rising to the surface to help make
Genoa lock, he sank slowly and the current and wheel wash
gently rolled him over in the soft mud at the bottom of the
river.

And honey when you come home on the train
please don't buy anything to drink, will you
try it this once for me? I wish you wouldn't
have even one drink when you get here honey.
— A LETTER FROM HOME

19

THE ONLY trouble with the economy size tube of
shaving cream is that it takes up more room in the valise
than a pair of rubber boots. I had one bust in my suitcase
one time and I would as soon have had a coconut cream
pie in with my shirts. Herb claimed once he was going to
invent some brushless shaving cream that would also go
good on crackers.

Anyway it was 5:40 A.M. and Diamond and Vincent, the wiper, and I were all shaving out of the same dirty bowl, and most of the time live steam was coming out of the faucet instead of hot water.

"You reckon Shorty'll come up?" Vincent said.

"He'll come up when he's ready," I said.

"Sometimes they don't come up for a long time," Diamond said.

"I bet he comes up within a week," I said.

"Get your elbow down, for chrissake," Vincent said.

I got into my new Key Imperial bib overalls and shoved out the screen door onto the deck. A little mist was hanging on the water near the shore. It still smelled hot from yesterday, and it must have been a sleepless night for a lot of people on Railroad Avenue. A fish took a stab at a fly and flopped back with a splash. The sun was already beginning to sizzle the whole wide valley. I went aft to the messroom.

After breakfast and the chorus of Hoople chomping noises I got my cap and gloves and went up to the foredeck and sat down on the double bitts for a smoke. The rest of the guys were sitting around on the lines and rigging.

"Where was you at when he went over?" Joe asked.

"I better go up to the printing shop at La Crosse and have this story printed up," I said. "God damn it, I was right behind him."

"That don't sound like Shorty to trip over the lock line. What was you guys doing, wrastling?"

"No, god damn it, we wasn't wrastling. He was going to check the starboard running light and I was behind him and about to go check the port one. He tripped over the god

[186]

damn lock line and fell over the head. I didn't shoot him, slug him, hit him with an ax or push him neither."

"Well you don't needa get sore about it," Joe said. "That must be a grand feeling, when you whack your head on them steel bottom plates and know you're gonna drownd."

"Yeh, grand," Diamond said.

Nobody said any more about it.

"Well," Joe said, "Cap he wants us to run ahead to La Crosse and see if we can find a deckhand. Then we gotta cut a new jackstaff, too. Bill, you come with me — and Diamond, you clean up the pilothouse and stand by here."

I got the gas can and filled it from the barrels on the stern, and we lowered the yawl into the river. Joe got in and commenced to tickle and squeeze the outboard and otherwise put it in an agreeable mood. The Chief came out and gave advice, but it wouldn't start so we took it in the engine room and pounded it for a while until it would go.

The cook gave me a dollar for cigars and then we were off and went dashing upstream alongside the barges, and I could see Sargent's head above the pilothouse windows.

I sat in the bow to keep her down and we cleared the head of the tow and could see the running lights still burning in their boxes where the other watch had forgot to take them in. It was about 6:30 A.M. by now and the sun was hot already and the birds were up and about; the crows had gone back inland but the redwing blackbirds were going strong and the swallows were skimming around near the shore. The boat and barges dropped behind as we came up the shore by the rock riprap and then headed into a crossing to the other side, toward Root River Upper Light, and way upriver you could see a big white chimney above the trees, the first sight of La Crosse.

Joe and I would look at each other and nod and holler, neither hearing the other above the roar of the outboard, and point at drift logs, or at a blue heron or the ripple from a fish jumping, or an airplane way up in the blue sky. That tough Joe had a silly look on his face, he was feeling so good — my how those mates loved to get the yawl out and run the outboard; for my part you can take all the outboards in Christendom and ship them to Missoula.

After a while we came up past Sand Slough Daymark and Sand Slough Light and went around all the black buoys in the big bend over to Broken Arrow and came up close to the bank by Broken Arrow and looked through the islands under the trees and it looked quiet and peaceful in there, and probably lousy with squirrels and ground hogs and mosquitoes. Then we passed the little slough that goes into Target Lake and headed up on the La Crosse Bridge and held her out in the middle. The city of La Crosse spread out on the Wisconsin side with Heileman's Brewery, home of Old Style Lager, and the warehouses and church steeples rising up in the pale summer sky. We tied up at the landing and we were about four miles ahead of the boat.

Every time I go ashore from a steamboat it seems like the first time. Now it seemed like a year since I had set my foot on a sidewalk and I was taking in everything like a kid at the County Fair, including the stray dogs, the telephone poles, and the candy wrappers in the gutters.

"Check on your Ingersoll, Bill," Joe said. "We must have about an hour on them."

A STRETCH ON THE RIVER

We started walking up through the brick streets to Main Street and a lot of the buildings down by the river had those old-time store fronts with cast-iron columns and names like LINKBETTER BLDG 1882 in cut limestone up at the top. Nowadays they are not stores any more but cheap warehouses for the uptown stores and upstairs they are flats for about twelve bucks a month. A little kid about five was sitting in the gutter with his baby sister who looked like she had just been pulled out of a ditch after a heavy rain, and they were playing with an empty pork and bean can and some pebbles. I slipped the little guy a nickel.

"Well, Rockefeller," says Joe, "what's the idea of that?" I asked him if he had such a swell time when he was five. "By god," he said, and went back and gave the kid a dime.

"That's how you can tell we're back to civilization again," I said.

"How's that?"

"As soon as you see a couple of pale kids with maybe an open sore on the face playing in a gutter while the old lady is over at the tavern, you know you're back."

"You're a god damn cynic, that's what you are."

"Listen, wherever I go I see people making a hash of life. Working at it overtime. I'm used to that. Let them puke their lives away if they want to. But there's too many kids around with nothing for Christmas but another slice of ham sausage and a swat on the ear."

"You should see some of the things I seen in St. Louis, and in Memphis."

"I've seen them, buddy, from here to Asia Minor."

"I'm glad this trip uptown is making you so cheerful."

[189]

"Well, let's go get a drink, Mister Mate," I said.

The sun was bouncing off the beautiful old limestone façades and a few farm trucks with home-style lettering on their cabs were looking for the feed store.

We went up a side street to a tavern called the Bumblebee. It was locked up but Joe said "Wait out here" and went into an entry beside the tavern. Next door was a grocery store and I looked at the pyramids of cut-rate cream-style corn stacked up in the window and a fat kid came out with a bucket to wash the windows.

"What do they call you up at school?" I said.

"Fat," he replied.

"That's what I thought," I said. "I bet you have a little guy in your class they call Peewee. How about it?"

"Naw, he's in sixth grade," he said.

Joe came out of the entry and I went over and pretty soon somebody came and unlocked the door of the tavern and we went in. The chairs were up on the tables and it was damp. It smelled of beer. "Never let your place get to smelling of beer," Papa used to say. His places smelled of polished mahogany, of starched shirts, of cigars, of rye bread, girls, Wisconsin cheese, Lucky Tiger hair tonic, of calfskin shoes, Old Hickory, Hennessy — but never of beer.

Joe and I went over to the bar and the bartender went under at the far end, put his shirt on and came down to where we were assuming Wm. S. Hart poses.

"Ace, this here is Bill Joyce. One of my boys off the boat," Joe said. That's what I was — one of Joe's boys. I wondered if dream puss up in St. Paul considered me her boy.

"Hiya," the bartender said. The trouble with this bar

so far was there were no girls in it. There was the prospect of a drink, however.

"How's Agnes?" Joe said.

"Same old Agnes," Ace said. "She'll likely be down in a while. I told her it was you."

Ace looked like the kind of boy who would wear French silk neckties, those terrible looking mudpies that cost $7.50.

"Gimme a slug of hundred proof, and a bottle of Old Style Lager," Joe said.

"Just wait while I get on my tie," Ace said. He went up to the back end of the bar and came back tying a French watered-silk necktie.

"Wow," Joe said. "Where'd that tie originate at?"

"No cracks now. I gave ten dollars for that on Michigan Boulevard."

"Tell him if it's worth it, Bill," Joe said.

"Sure," I said. "That's French silk."

"This boy of mine," Joe said, "he knows about all there is."

"This boy of yours wants a drink," I said.

"Speak and you shall be served," said Ace.

"Philadelphia and a bottle of Grain Belt," I said.

The bartender set down the two bottles of beer and the shot glasses.

"How is this Joe to work for?" he said comically. "Pretty mean, I'll bet, ain't he? Gives you a hard time, don't he?"

"He's hell, but I can handle him," I said.

Joe laughed and the bartender poured.

"Here's to Shorty," Joe said.

"God love him," I said.

"Wait," says Ace. "Who's Shorty?"

"One of the boys. He got drownded last night."

"God rest his soul, poor kid," said the bartender, and we threw down our whiskeys and placed the cold bottles to our lips and took long, long gulps of that beautiful beer.

Life grew more vibrant when the beer and whiskey hit bottom. We talked about the war and the river and wages. On the bar was last night's paper: *Yanks Make New Gains in North Sicily.*

"Don't your conscience hurt you none?" Ace said. He spread the paper out on the bar with the headline toward us.

"Mine ain't exactly killing me," Joe said. "How's yours, Bill?"

"OK," I said. "Mine gives me a little twinge once in a while. Nothing that hard work won't cure."

"Explain this to me, Ace," Joe said. "You got a job ashore so you must necessarily have more brains than me. What's the big reason Bill and me should get into the army?"

"Why, ain't you got no patriotism?"

"I don't know much about that. You got any, Bill?"

"I got a lot of Bill patriotism," I said.

"Listen, all the guys that's in, want out. Am I right?" Joe said.

"That ain't got nothing to do with it," Ace said.

"No? It's got everything to do with it as far as Joe Denckman is concerned. I been underdog all my life. I ain't in no mood to begin all over again eatin it with a spoon like I did for years off all the hard old mates I worked for. I ain't ready for it, boy. No I ain't."

"Me, I'm dead set on the advantages of being alive," I said. "I can't think of hardly a thing in the world I consider worth being dead for. Especially when the country is overloaded with alive fools getting elected to Congress."

"Youse are hopeless," Ace said, and poured me another Philadelphia.

"And as far as that big long sleep is concerned, why I'm feeling wide awake," I said, "I ain't a bit sleepy."

"Listen, hotrocks," Joe said, "whadda you think we're doing out there, playing duck on a rock? How come we get deferred? It's as plain as can be they got to have the coal moved. And just about twice as plain that if they took us river rats off our jobs they'd never find any other mutts ignorant enough to work the hours we work for the crummy wages we get."

"Sing them blues, boy," I said. "Listen to him, Ace, his boilers are beginning to jump. Pour him out another of them conscience builders."

"It ain't as though we wasn't doing nothing for the country, like as if we was tending bar, for example," Joe said.

"Now was that a friendly remark?" Ace said. "What if everybody felt like you guys? You got a poor attitude."

"Attitude my ass," Joe said.

The door from upstairs opened and Agnes appeared. She was in a white satin housecoat with big red roses all over it. She was built big, for the second row of the line in the Mutual Burlesk, with her fine strong breasts, plump arms, and a smile that showed she liked men.

"Yeah, what if everybody thought like you guys?" Ace said.

"If everybody thought like me," I said, "the world would probably be even more peculiar than it is."

"Hello, Joe," Agnes said. "Where you been all summer? What you been doing?"

"I been breathing in and out," Joe said.

"You might of come in to see us once in a while."

"Ag, I ain't been ashore here but once this season, and that was at 4 A.M."

"Next time it's 4 A.M. come on up. Maybe my man Valentino here will be in Madison on one of his *business* trips."

"Say, ain't you putting on a little weight, honey?" Joe said.

"Ha ha," says Ace.

"You shut your face, bulldog," says Agnes.

"You look a lot better," Joe said. "You was too skinny before."

"This is better than vaudeville," Ace said.

"Joe, we gotta push off," I said.

"That's swell," she said, and poured herself a wineglass of orange gin. "I come in the room and right away your boss here says you gotta go."

"I don't own the barge line yet, Ag," Joe said. "I just work on her. For my part I'd as soon stay here all day. How about it, boss?"

"It's forty minutes already," I said.

"One more and we'll go."

Everything seemed so simple now. There were Papa and Herb at home and a lot of money, high-power cars, custom-made suits and big parties, and up at St. Paul there was

[194]

Merle, a girl with a heavenly nose, six dresses, a suit, and a ninety-dollar fur coat. I was in the middle, at La Crosse, and the thing to do was to go up in a balloon and see if I could see St. Paul, or order champagne, buy a gun and shoot up the town, go flower picking, write some poetry, or take a nap in the long grass waving on the summit of some Mississippi bluff.

And then we were outside again.

"This is a bum deal," I said. "Here we are out in the street again and Agnes is back inside."

"Yeah," Joe said. "Come on, let's go over to the drugstore. I gotta get some shaving cream."

"The economy size, no doubt," I said.

We want girls for sweethearts, so that when
we get an arm shot off, or are kicked by a
mule, or thrown from a bucking horse and are
laid away for repairs, we may hear a gentle
voice and see the glitter of a crystal tear . . .
                        — DURANGO *Record*
                        Durango, Colorado
                        March 12, 1881

20

JEHOVAH had created another fine day of golden
sunshine free of charge, and I felt the way a chicken hawk
must feel, floating away up so high above the fields while
even the cottontails are having their troubles down below.
I had a letter from Merle in purple ink folded in my shirt
pocket, and except for a hole in the toe of my left sock I

was as happy as an American can be without several charge accounts. All these crummy river towns were home to me and Joe — I had eaten in all their cafés, drunk in all their bars, slept in all their hotels, loved all their girls, sat in all their parks, waited in all their depots, sat on all their curbstones — and they don't have the Golden Gate or the subway, but all the same you take the picturesque, rundown New England towns such as you see in *Life* magazine and I'll take any town from Jefferson Barracks to the Falls of St. Anthony. While we're at it, you take my quota of frozen daiquiris, Château Yquem, and vintage Scotch highballs with pin-point carbonation and I'll take a shot or two of American whiskey with a cold bottle of beer, and let's not wait till five o'clock to get at it; let's have it right now, while the receiving clerks are opening the return goods down at the jobbing house and the steno is giving the other girls a description of the box of candy Leroy gave her last night.

"What's the deal there on Agnes?" I said.

"Don't trouble your pretty head, William," Joe said. "That's a dummy run, boy. Strictly a dummy run."

"Yeah? Well, she looked like she wanted to sprinkle a little sugar on you and eat you for breakfast," I said.

"Don't never let them appearances deceive you," said Joe.

We did a quick turn into the drugstore and I got some White Owls for the cook and some newspapers and the *N. Y. Mirror* Sunday edition and a copy of *Screenland* and *Blue Beetle* for the boys and some razor blades and a postcard of the bridge and some Black Sea cigarette papers and

a comb and two Cocoanut Mounds bars and a package of
Black Jack; then we hightailed it for the landing and set
our plunder in the bow and shoved off. The boat and barges
were downstream about half a mile plodding along so
slowly they seemed not to be moving at all.

"We'll run on up to Minnesota Island and cut that
jackstaff," Joe said, giving the outboard a kick. "Start, you
ornery bastard!"

That suited me. We could have taken off for the Falkland
Islands after that jackstaff for all I cared. A light south wind
had come up and the sun was sparkling on the little waves,
as clear and bright as a jewelry store window, minus the
price tags. I was still up in the blue sky, floating a mile
above town.

"You no-good, useless morphidite," Joe said conversa-
tionally to the motor.

The outboard responded with a blast that rattled the
glassware in the Hotel Duluth and we dashed off up the
great historic waterway. Joe screwed up his face and delivered me an inscrutable wink. On up past Pettibone Park,
where the lovers come to park in the evening and unbutton
and unhook each other, and on up the channel, dodging the
nun buoys, throwing a wash on the sand bars, scaring the
fish out of six weeks' growth, devastating the peace of
the morning with our internal combustion.

Joe pointed ahead and I looked upstream. The west span
of the Milwaukee railroad drawbridge was jammed with
barges coming down dead slow. We passed the two black
buoys and went up through the east span of the open draw.
It was the *Pat Hurley*, rolling her wheel listlessly until she

[199]

would be clear of the bridge and start beating up the water again; the engineer was back on the fantail beside the mammoth pitman, which rose and fell slowly. The mess-boy came out of the galley and threw a bucket of potato peels overboard.

We cut up past the black buoys and crossed over to Minnesota Island, ran her in and tied off to a cottonwood root. I took the ax and we climbed up the bank and walked under the trees; it was soft and warm and smothery in there, with the smell of mud and burdock leaves, nettles, wild grapevines, bugs and sink holes, a few flowers, rotten logs, pregnant toadstools, and the mosquitoes, who greeted us with a long cheer for the team. Although the Ford Hopkins drugstore was only a few miles away, and from under the still trees we could see the semi-trailer trucks burning up the slab across the river on their way to Winona, here on our musky island it was tangled and wild, and the cottonwoods and elms, existing only for the pleasure of the bluejays who frolicked in their upper branches, were poised like lithographic, old-fashioned trees overburdened with foliage. Under the loose bark of dead trees the bugs pursued their dismal calling, while in the rich alluvium underfoot blind worms slid sightlessly on moist and endless errands. As it was in the beginning, it is now and ever shall be, world without end, regardless of the RKO Orpheum circuit.

We walked across the jungly island and on the far side, by the sweet stagnant slough, a big gar pike lay stranded in the shore mud, with his long snout desiccating in the summer sun and his soul in hell. Beyond, with the salamanders creeping stupidly among their roots, the lotus bloomed and filled the air with whiffs of the ancient Nile. God, Mohammed, or Zoroaster perhaps could give a complete inventory of what lay beneath the surface of that wide and slimy pool, and if any of them knew I hoped they would keep it to themselves. A water snake went horribly squirming through the green plankton.

"Now I know where to bring the body next time I kill somebody," Joe said, heaving a dead limb at the snake. It hit him square and he died frothing.

"Do the Cards know you're loose?" I said.

Leaving the fringe-finned ganoids and the earthly remains of gar pike and snake, we went away from the hot prehistoric expanse of trapped water and made our way back through the whirring insects to the shaded alleys beneath the trees. Clubbing a path through the nettles and eager undergrowth, we came at last to a half-open, park-like place beside the river, where the trunks of the trees rose high in search of the sun, and the shade restricted the ground cover to sickly grasses and pale flowers.

There was an old fisherman's camp in there, with a shanty up on stilts to keep it above the high water. We combed it over but there was nothing there except a busted Dietz lantern, a pair of old rubber boots with holes, and some rusted-out tin plates. A 1926 coal and ice dealer's calendar was hanging behind the door — no wonder there was not much left. Joe was set on getting something though, so he took along an old file he found in the weeds.

We picked out a good straight elm about twenty-five feet

high. Joe grabbed the ax and commenced to work out some
of his high spirits on it, and the chips began to fly. A blue
racer slid for cover into the brush. The tree gave up and
came down with a swish.

"There's more mosquitoes here than cardinals at Judge
Ryan's funeral," Joe said. "Let's get out of here."

We stripped the tree and dragged the pole over to the
river; it didn't set so good on the boat, so we decided to
tow it out when the boat came along. She was just heading
through the drawbridge, about a mile down river, her eight
loads setting down low in the water and creeping along
against the current. We sat down on the bank and had a
smoke and cooled off and we talked about whether snakes
were good to have around a farm or not. I told Joe there was
no such thing as a hoop snake, but he said his uncle saw
one down in Illinois on his farm.

"When he seen my uncle coming he just tucked that
ole tail in his mouth and rolled down the hill as slick as a
whistle," Joe said.

"Next thing you'll be telling me that one about the catfish that swallowed the poodle dog," I said.

Across the fluttering water at River Junction a big Milwaukee freight was heading up the line with about seventy-
five cars from all over — the Nickel Plate, the Erie, the Pere
Marquette, the Seaboard Airline, Canadian National, D &
R G W, Vermont Central, B & O, Boston and Maine.

"I never would of believed it neither," said Joe, "until my
uncle seen it with his own eyes."

"Is he the same one lived in that house down back of

Clarksville in Pike County where the ghosts kept slamming doors all night and milking the cows?" I said.

"That's him," said Joe.

"OK," I said. "If he saw it, it must be so. He sure as hell couldn't be wrong."

"Ah, you and your education. That must take most of the pleasure out of life."

We tied a line on the elm pole and turned loose and towed it out into the channel. Sargent saw us coming and gave a toot on the whistle to get the deckhands off their asses, and we landed up by the head of the barges. Diamond was out there — it was strange to see him out there without Shorty — and I tossed him our line and we flopped alongside. I got up on the barges and Diamond and I hauled the new jackstaff aboard and dumped it across the coal piles, and then led the yawl back to the boat, hooked up the bridle and cranked it aboard with the winch.

Diamond got a handful of rope yarn and I swiped a dirty towel and got a hammer and nails and we went out on the head of the tow and nailed the towel on top of the elm tree for a flag. Then we pulled off a hatch cover and shoved the pole in and tied it to the ladder. Rescued from the oblivion of the jungle, the lucky tree began its career as a wanderer.

Joe climbed up the iron stairs and went in the pilothouse and gave Captain Sargent the newspapers.

"Well," Sargent said. "No deckhand."

"Naw," Joe said. "I couldn't find none."

Sargent looked over the front page. "Well, I see that

guy killed his wife and three kids they didn't ketch him yet."

"How's that new jackstaff suit you?" Joe said.

"A big improvement," Sargent said, and he blew a long and a short for Dresbach lock; steering by the elm tree with the fluttering towel on it, he got in shape to enter.

*"How is it, Frank, that you who are rich, and
the heir of a large fortune, have become the
friend of a poor boy like me?"*

*"I go with you, Herbert, because I like
you."*

— HORATIO ALGER, JR., *Making His Way*

21

NOBODY around the old home town thinks very
highly of the boys who have found things too slow and
gone off where the lights burn a little brighter. But sailors
irritate the Main Street bunch the most. Deep sea, inland,
or submarine, all sailors are under suspicion because they
are never around for the Community Chest drive and even

when they do spend some time inside the city limits they are likely to say something rude to the president of the Second National Bank instead of telling him he is big stuff.

They got Jack Darling up to the Kiwanis one time to give them a talk about life at sea. What a talk. He was home off the Isthmian Line to bury his mother and had been spending a good deal of time drinking wine, beer, and anything else he could lay his hands on.

"How the hell do you guys stand it?" he said when urged to orate. "Last month I was in Dublin Me. and the Bos'n was out near Phoenix Park on a party with a couple of live ones. Next month I'll be in Melbourne. I s'pose you boys will still be setting here looking satisfied at each other. Oh mama, what a way to live. Say, I'll send all you big shots a postcard of Capetown, OK?"

And so on until he got thirsty and went out to look for a drink. The Reverend G. Parks Alexander had a fit and old man Watson, the sawdust king, described the affair as an outrage. Papa was there and he said it was an outrage all right — nobody even offered Jackie a drink.

That's the way the boys are. They are a different breed.

I have known all kinds of sailors, and in general I'll say they are more interesting than normal people. They are mostly unpredictable in their behavior and hence seldom boring. Your average landlubber on the other hand is a bore. Never having been anyplace he naturally has nothing new to talk about after he is twelve years old.

Most sailors will take a chance. They are usually weak

on French poetry and Byzantine history but have an open mind. They live pretty close to the edge of things and can spot a phony at a hundred yards. They are always pressed for time and have to get started right away with women.

But anyway, for a drugstore cowboy I had sure taken to the river. Papa didn't get it at all. He couldn't figure it out.

"It's a transferral of intent. It's a result of childhood trauma. It's Oedipus denial," said my sister-in-law, who was beautiful, thank god, so you could put up with this spinach.

"I think it's necrophilia rejection," said Herb, making his wife mad. "But maybe Bill just likes it."

And meantime we forged ahead in search of a plot, through the sunny summer days on the Upper Mississippi, but nothing happened. The Burlington trains ran up and down on the east side of the river and the Milwaukee trains on the west side. The sun came up in Wisconsin and set in Minnesota. We met the *Tri-Cities*, all white and neat, bringing her empty gasoline barges downstream, the *Lucinda Clark*, the *Mokita*, the *Bob Tresler* (an old steam stern-wheeler strayed from the Ohio River), the *Wheelock Whitney* with her pilothouse on top of the pilothouse and her tall stacks, and Captain Savage came out on the bridge and gave us a wave. We passed Queens Bluff, six hundred feet sheer from the water line, and crossed the valley to lock through at Trempealeau, under the big rocky fortress that caused so many passionate paragraphs of descriptive writing by the nineteenth-century reporters. We dropped a load at the power plant in Winona and went on up the river with seven, around the bend at Betsy Slough and Pap Chute, past Fountain City sound asleep and snoring under the big hill, and Minneiska, and beautiful Alma, and Grand Encampment, and Teepeeota, and Wabasha, where the cute little steamer *Aquila* lay at the bank waiting for an invitation to raise steam and go to work. And then we passed the Chippewa River mouth, and Reads Landing, where the raftsmen used to wait for the logs, and fill in the time with drink, comic stories, and murder. And then we entered Lake Pepin, the cook made peach shortcake, and we dropped another load at Lake City in the twilight while vacation trippers stood on the shore in sport shirts and watched our picturesque behavior. No, there is not much plot to the Upper Mississippi. First the ice goes out and everybody goes to the river to watch the floes sliding past town, and within a week or two the first boy of the season gets drowned in a leaky skiff and below town the first steamboat blows for the railroad drawbridge. And then if you are working on the steamboats, there is the whole summer stretching ahead — bounded on the south by St. Louis, on the north by St. Paul, on each side by the romantic bluffs, islands, and river towns, and overhead by the high blue sky. There are sunsets and little river towns at dawn. And there is the river at night. And work. And pork chops, pie, fried potatoes and bright red Jello. And there is sleep, the kind of sleep that comes from hard work and no conscience.

All these things are good for the soul. The soul is a commodity we don't hear so much about since the radio and gas engine took over the country, but in the right atmosphere it flourishes even today. Joe had one. It had a few holes in it but it was still serviceable.

With all this we had, too, our trials and struggles, our

Cape Horn, our typhoons, our doldrums. We had enough evidences of divine intent. We had death and disillusionment. We had sermons from the blackbirds and exhortations from the willow trees. Satan was with us to be balked. And beneath us at the bottom of the river the current rolled over the slime of purgatory.

But of plot we had no more than the usual question that follows every man from the Third Ward School to the final waxy appearance at the funeral home: *What shall I do?* What next? Shall I buy some shoes? Shall I make love or go to Wichita? How beautiful a morning, but there's always evening coming. Shall I give myself and my two-pants suit and my ugly temper and my old leather wallet containing thirty-two dollars in bills to some girl, or keep these personal treasures for myself? In that case how much of myself shall I give to anybody? Perhaps I could write a poem. Maybe I should have been a doctor. Am I a man or a butterfly dreaming of being a man? Listen to the train whistle blow. A pension in twenty years for the fireman.

After we dropped our barge at Lake City we backed out and headed up the lake again. The breeze blew in from Wisconsin for a change, from Green Bay or Ashland. We had six loads now and would make better time from here on in. St. Paul was still seventy miles away upstream.

"This is where old Johnny Plummer jumped overboard," Joe said as we sat between the barges at the second coupling and watched the shore lights.

"What was his trouble?" I said.

"Whiskey. He lived on it. He went crazy right in here abreast of Maiden Rock one evening. Shoved the window back and jumped off the bridge hollering bloody murder. Never come up. Never did find him."

"Snakes."

"Yeah."

"Joe," I said, "I think I'll be a pilot."

"Are you outa your head?" Joe said. "Why, with your education . . ."

"Listen, Joe, let's leave my education out of it just this once. I got kicked out of the only good school I ever went to."

"Yeh — but you and your brother and your old man, why you really cut some ice down there at home."

"I'm a small town sport, that's what I am. My old man is a saloonkeeper and my brother married a bank roll."

"Ah, you make me sick."

"I think I'll hang around just the same. You know, work is a novelty to me. I haven't got a friend outside the Inland Barge Line that ever put in a day's work."

"Well, it ain't no novelty to me."

Across the lake a passenger train blew for the crossing and glided down the shore past Stockholm. We were eight days out of Alton, and that train would be in Chicago in just five or six hours.

"No, Lord God, it ain't no novelty to me," Joe said.

"And another thing I got to settle is that St. Paul matter," I said.

"Boy, I sure fixed you up when I innerduced you to that baby doll. I sure did."

"We'll be in St. Paul tomorrow night this time," I said.

[210]

"If we don't get hung up, and if Sargent don't take a dive like Johnny Plummer we will."

"How do you like that girl?" I said. Another boat was coming down; Sargent exchanged passing signals with the searchlights.

"She's a good looker."

"What else?"

"I don't know nothing else about her except what I can see. Man, that's a byoodiful girl."

"Yeah. That's a fact," I said. "She's a killer, boy."

"What kinda performer is she?" Joe asked.

"She's hot," I said, "and artistic."

"That's swell, kid," Joe said. "Suppose you two champs get married. What you gonna do when you get tired rehearsing? You gotta come out into the daylight sometime. Can this here wonder girl bake a pie?"

"Pie. I can get along without pie."

"All right then," Joe said. "How about her and this rich brother of yours? How they gonna clash it off?"

"Oh my god."

"And your buddies back home. This here Schwartz with all the money. What'll he think of her? And them Watsons that you say owns the town. What's she gonna do when you innerduce her to old lady Watson and them girls? Swallow her gum?"

"They're just a bunch of vulgar rich people."

"Yeah — but they don't know it," Joe said.

"The hell with them," I said.

I went across the barge and watched the other tow pass,

the barges looming up in the night, and then the towboat, with the engine room all brightly lighted and two engineers leaning against the door jamb. The pilot gave a snort on the air whistle, snapped on the pilothouse light and waved across.

"What boat is it?" Joe said.

"Looks like the *Celeste*," I said. "But she doesn't run up in here."

"That's her, just the same," Joe said.

Now we were abreast of Frontenac and coming up on Point-No-Point and Wacouta and the end of the lake. The lake is just a wide place in the river, a geologic curiosity of some kind. The channel is buoyed out at the upper end and then cuts through some stumps and dead trees and you are back in the river again. There are some sharp bends and the forest is very thick on both sides and the river is beginning to narrow down. You pass the State Farm to port and then you are at Red Wing, Minnesota, another moldy and wonderful old river town. From Red Wing in to the Twin Cities it is almost like a different river. It is narrow, and the bottom is rock. You see native white pine. The closer you get to St. Paul, the smaller the river gets. At Pine Bend and Robinsons Rocks the river looks more like the coast of Maine than the Mississippi. In these upper reaches of navigation on the Mississippi I always felt as though we were almost to Hudson Bay or the Great Slave Lake.

The *Celeste* passed, and her range lights faded down the lake toward Lake City point. She was from New Orleans, exactly 1759.4 miles downstream.

"That's the *Celeste*, all right," Joe said. "And she's got a long long ways to Canal Street."

"Now that you come to mention it," I said, "I wonder if she could bake a pie. And I wonder if she would want an aluminum Christmas tree instead of a real one, and if a lot of nutty relatives would show up from Grand Forks or Fargo."

"They all got relatives. Where does she come from?"

"Up in the iron range. Someplace up back of Duluth where the snow gets thirty feet deep."

What flavors of warmth and seduction I could remember from my other life, before I had commenced to live, before I had lain in bed beside the girl from the iron range, listening to her breathe in the early morning hours. I could remember the girls from Brookline, the sheer stockings from R. H. Stearns, the swelling white piqué shirtwaists, holding hands on 52nd Street, the whispers of Southern coeds on spring nights. And the smell of the leather seats on my phaeton, and lobster thermidor, and girls with very expensive voices.

"It's funny," Joe said. "Them people from Duluth and the iron range consider St. Paul is way down south."

And then that college I went to. I learned one thing anyway: if you're not clever to start with, college won't cure the condition. That's contrary to another cherished American belief.

"Were you ever in Duluth?" I asked.

"No, I never was," Joe said. "Hey, where you going,

hoss?" he added to Diamond, who had appeared, strolling out between the barges.

"I'm gonna check them runnin lights," Diamond answered, pausing at the coupling to light a cigarette and kick the fore and aft wires.

"You know what you need, hoss, you need a girl. Why don't you go out in St. Paul and get a girl so's you'll have something to look forward to when we get up in this country?"

"I don't think so," Diamond said.

"If you have a girl in St. Paul, why when you get the first whiff of the packing houses it's like roses in the lane."

"I'm slow with girls," Diamond said, and he continued on out between the barges to check the running lights.

"Now I ask you, Bill, what would you do if you couldn't get some regular?" Joe said.

"I would end it all with a dull knife," I said.

"Pathetic, ain't it? Can you beat it?"

"It's about 65 per cent of life," I said. "If it's really good I'd rate it even higher."

However, it should be restricted to poets, like Joe and me. Some substitute should be devised and rationed out to the undeserving. The undeserving would include people who sell insurance and those who tell stories in dialect. This would narrow the field considerably because almost everybody you meet nowadays is an insurance man who wants to give you a little leatherette notebook free.

"Well, no, I never was in Duluth," Joe said, breaking the

record for picking up forgotten threads of the conversation. "Was you?"

"Uh huh," I said. "I used to go up there when I was a kid to visit my aunt."

Aunt Pauline's house in Duluth. Ah, poet, do you remember the dark rich parlor that smelled of varnish, the plush chairs, and Herb reading the *Erie Train Boy* out loud? Do you remember the gold dinner plates and Uncle Victor's cigars?

When I sat up in front with Faber, the chauffeur, in the big Minerva town car, there was a funny smell. Faber had been waiting to pick me up at the children's party and had probably been whiling away the time in a speak-easy; it was his breath, the funny smell. I sat there looking at the dash clock, holding the piece of party cake in its tissue paper wrapping, and I began to feel sick.

"Enough is enough," beautiful Aunt Pauline said to Mama in the hallway. "Victor simply must give him his walking papers this time."

"You couldn't mistake it," Mama said.

"Oh lord," said Aunt Pauline, for leaning pensively against the carved halltree I had inclined slightly forward and projected fragments of birthday party on the parquet floor.

They put me to bed and Aunt Pauline gave me a spoonful of something dreadful. "I'll read *John Martin's Book* to you after supper," she said. She was a beautiful big blonde such as they do not make any more. She was a real beauty and smelled lovely all the time. Mama was a brunette, and almost as pretty as Aunt Pauline, and played the grand piano in a velvet dress.

The fog came in from Lake Superior as I lay under the silk puff in Mama's room, and the foghorn on the breakwater began to moan, and evening came. Faber locked up the carriage house garage and I heard him whistling as he went down the steep sidewalk toward Superior Street. Pretty soon Greta or one of the maids would bring me some milk toast and after supper maybe I could get up and listen to Herb's crystal set. And Aunt Pauline had promised to read. Downstairs Mama was playing the piano. I thought of the great ice-cold lake with the ore freighters hove-to in the fog, and listened to the foghorns blowing.

That was Aunt Pauline's house in Duluth.

"What aunt was that?" Joe said.

"My mother's sister Pauline."

"Your mother's sister?"

"Yeah, Aunt Pauline. She married Victor Rosenthal, a big shot in the iron range."

"Your aunt married somebody named Rosenthal! He's a Jew ain't he?"

"A hundred per cent," I said. "Maybe more."

"He's your uncle, is that it?"

"My Uncle Victor."

"All the nights we sat around out here together on the barges. How come you never mentioned him before?"

"Why should I? I haven't seen him in twenty years."

"Rosenthal. I'll be god damned."

The sky was filled with a million stars and I was filled with sadness. Why did I have to bring all that up? Much

[216]

better to think of work and the river and the nearness of St. Paul, of prize fighting and movie stars, or parties where Kools are indicated for throat protection. Duluth was all gone, Victor Rosenthal was gone, Aunt Pauline gone, Mama gone — only the Spalding Hotel and the foghorns blowing in the winter dusk remained. And now here was a girl down out of the iron range to drive me crazy; her old man probably worked at one of Uncle Victor's mines.

I should have gone home right then and married Adele, Bunny, Francine, or Claire — none of them knew anything much and each had a father with a large car and real estate. I could settle down with the sport page and the wife could call up a girl friend and describe her new shade of lipstick and what she told the maid about coming in late.

"Rosenthal's rich too, I suppose," Joe said.

"Everybody in the family is lousy with money," I said. "Uncle Victor doesn't get any pleasure out of his any more, though."

"He don't? Why not?"

"He jumped out a window about fourteen years ago."

"You got the damnedest family. My uncles all just raise kids and get the crops in. Yours jump out windows, get shot by gangsters, eaten by cannibals — I don't know what all."

"All your relations come from out in the sticks. They go to bed early and stay out of trouble."

"You oughta write a book, kid."

"This is where I came in. I'll meet you at the Coney Island Lunch across the street."

"I ain't kidding. It would be all right."

"Joe, in everybody's home town there are several people that wear funny clothes and have no income and they are writing a book. They have been writing this god damn book for fifteen years. They don't know anything. They think they're too artistic to work. And as far as writing a book, they'd have a better chance getting ahead in the shipping department down at the licorice factory. But oh no, they're writing a book. If all the books that are being written in towns under fifty thousand were published, why we'd have to colonize Greenland to make room."

"Well, that was quite a blast," says Joe. "I'm glad to see you take something serious in life besides gash."

"That's what old man Watson, the president of the mill, used to tell Papa all the time. 'You ought to write a book, Dan,' he used to say. 'You know — the Capones, Torrio, and all that. With your, um, unconventional slant on things I'd bet it'd sell like hot cakes.' 'Why don't you write one instead, George?' Papa would say. 'You know more crooks in the lumber business than I ever knew as a bootlegger. For example, we worked by the law of supply and demand. Some of the boys may have tried to limit the supply by unorthodox methods involving firearms, but they didn't get together and fix prices.' 'Oh Dan, don't be such an idealist,' Watson would say. 'I'm not an idealist,' says Papa, 'that's just my, um, unconventional slant on things.'"

"This here Watson sounds like a bird," Joe said.

"He's a bird all right," I said. "Thanks to him and his old man and his gang, there's hardly a stick of timber left in the states of Minnesota and Wisconsin. But that's another story, and has practically nothing to do with my St. Paul problem."

"In another minute we'll be back to that pie again, or your Uncle Victor."

"Speaking of pie," I said, "let's go back to the boat and see if Harry left any out."

"At last you said something I can understand. Let's go."

Up ahead the lights of the Red Wing Highway Bridge dangled in the sky.

. . . wasn't that the best time, that time when we were young at sea; young and had nothing, on the sea that gives nothing, except hard knocks — and sometimes a chance to feel your strength . . .

— CONRAD

22

AT THE OUTER CITY LIMITS, below the city of St. Paul, a six-inch pipe hangs over the river and discharges a stream of crimson liquid into the Mississippi. This is one of the first intimations to the hard-working deckhand on any Upper River towboat of the imminence of The City. The pipe comes underground from one of the packing plants and the crimson liquid is blood.

It's a pretty good-sized stream and a rich bloody color, and I never cared much for this scenic wonder at all.

"Gory, ain't it," said the Second Mate.

"That's only a partial description," said the deckhand.

I have come into the city of St. Paul on summer nights when the trees on the back streets hung their leaves silently, and love was a very sticky affair — on afternoons in November when snow flurries swirled over the barges and the bilge pumps froze up — on very sad evenings when the evidence of the slaughterhouses hung in the air in front of the outlying drugstores, and horrid children sat on the curbstones poking with sticks.

But now we were passing through a bridge called the Belt Line Railroad Bridge at a place called Pigs Eye. Across the land and above the roofs of some riverside shanties the skyline of the city arose in a faint outline. The tower of the First National Bank Building quivered in the sky like a mirage. To look at this Maxfield Parrish vision of luxury and civilized delight you could forget that it was actually composed of Portland cement and base desires, of underground conduits filled with eggshells, blood, and cigar butts, of hairpins under rugs, plugged drains, cold bacon grease, artistically cosmetized corpses, rats that squeal and bite, the tears of young girls betrayed, carpets with worn places, unpleasant mattresses, the loneliness of old age, broken glass, defiled sidewalks, undesirable shoes, and all the "beautiful dreck" of the big city. You could forget it because of the stores filled with perfume and pink writing paper that you knew were also there. And there were multi-filament rayon crepe panties with blue ribbon inserts, and

[222]

pistachio bonbons, and silk umbrellas; and bars, warm and cozy in winter, cool in summer, where the drinks made you feel infinitely wise and very handsome; and there were hotels with room service and rental radios, where lovers (I myself for one) devoured each other with passion and played at water sports in the scented tub water. And on some days in the city the streets were filled with girlish kisses, and it rained strawberry pop. And someplace in this mess of masonry and gore was a girl with black hair, and round arms to hold me with.

It was late afternoon and Joe and Diamond and I were stripping the tow, carrying all the loose rigging back to the boat — the lock lines, the light boxes and stands, extra lashings and wires, junk line, the bilge pump, and any other loose gear lying around on the decks of the barges.

"You're crazy," said Joe, with a ratchet over his shoulder and the back of his shirt already wet with sweat in the late afternoon sun, "with this idea about being a pilot."

"Half the world is crazy along with me," I said, coming up behind him with a coiled-up lashing over my shoulder and two iron bars in my left hand. "It's just a question of point of view. Back home I'm not such a hot shot as I claim to be, I imagine. Look at the beautiful city of St. Paul rising in the sky out of this god damn wasteland, and quit worrying about me and my fate. Many a better man than me has turned his back on the twentieth century and gone to work."

"I've spent most of my life, ever since I left the farm, trying to get a place where I could get out of some work. That's why *I* aim to be a pilot."

"And that, my boy, is the whole trouble with this chrome-plated country of ours. Religion used to hold the people together. Now that's on the rocks. Work, good hard work, got us out of the jungle and into a Diesel towboat. But now, oh hell, everybody thinks work is degrading. All the high school boys want to be executives like Franchot Tone, they don't want to be carpenters or tailors or mates on a steamboat and get their hands dirty."

"Well, there's a lot of carpenters around."

"And most of them wish they were sitting behind a desk talking through the interoffice communication system. Why do you think we pulled off three timberheads on that brand-new barge last month? Those welders had a hell of a lot of pride in their profession, didn't they? I'm telling you, boy, work is the only thing left in the twentieth century to ennoble the mind of man, and in this country the most despised."

"You got quite a line of jive, ain't you? Well how about the tired businessman? What makes this guy so tired if he don't work?"

"Very simple, junior. Dr. Joyce will explain everything: the businessman has got a guilt complex because he don't do any work. The result is that he spends hours every day going through tedious and nerve-racking episodes of his own invention which have an appearance of work. These episodes are called sales meetings, panel discussions, top-management forums, long-range planning committees, idea clinics, personnel parleys — and they are guaranteed to depress and exhaust the mind of man worse than the thought of death. I've been there and I know. And the whole process

[224]

adds up to zero. You either have the brains to make it or you'll go broke. And that, Mister Mate, is why the great American businessman is so god damn tired. He could knock off at noon every day, but he has to prove to himself that he's working like hell because he is ashamed he isn't."

"Holy Jesus."

"Holy Jesus is clear out of the picture nowadays. He's got no message, no 'thought to inject here,' no slogan to offer at an idea clinic."

We reached the boat and Joe dropped his ratchet down on the steel deck with a crash. He fished his Duke's Mixture and Zig-Zags out of his breast pocket and rolled a cigarette as we went out again between the barges. Diamond came at us with a wire over his shoulder.

"As far as this job is concerned, there's more to it than that, too," I said. "I never had time to stop and look at things before. The river, and the islands, and — oh hell, the fish jumping in the morning, and the smell of the coal after an all-night rain, and the sunset bouncing off the rocks above Trempealeau lock."

"Quite a poet, ain't you?"

"Well, you Dutchman, what do you think of the Upper Mississippi? You're not just along here for the ride. You could have got some sermons from the earth riding the tractor back home, and got the farm for yourself someday. Shorty could have, but he had the steamboat fever, same as you. It's the big river, and going someplace, and the bluffs above Dubuque, and that crazy messboy, and the lights of St. Paul at night. It's being in St. Louis one day

[225]

and at Hannibal the next. It's Sargent and the coal and all the rest of it."

Dayton Bluff was ahead, and one of the streamliners from Chicago was coming in on a slow bell along the tracks under the bluff, with a full crew in the club car.

"You make this sound like a regular carnival," Joe said. "Let's hear some more about the river."

"All right. Keokuk lock. And those girls in Alton, Toots and Darlene. And that evening in Muscatine. And the bar in La Crosse. And Lake Pepin last night at sundown. Why man, just in this one trip we had more living than the average bird gets in a lifetime."

"Sing them blues, boy," Joe said. "You take half and I'll take the other half," and we picked up the lock line and started back again to the boat.

"Sure," I said, "business is swell if you're at the top like me and my brother. The money comes in and you go to the golf club and talk to a bunch of nuts that are worried about whether they can pay the next installment of dues. The banker is a bore and the big shots can't read and none of them has stopped to look at a robin hopping around on the lawn since they were ten years old. It's the berries, my friend. Two-tone shoes and big thick steaks."

"That's what I'd like right now, a big thick steak," Joe said. "But I can get along without the banker, if he's anything like the one back home."

"I'll guarantee he's the same if not worse. The whole breed is the same. I can't think of one I know that would make half a deckhand."

"I bet that would hurt their feelings to know that."

[226]

"Did you ever hear of a steamboat pilot with ulcers?" I said.

"I sure did, kid, old Captain Williams on the *North Star* ate so much baking soda we had it aboard by the case. And Sargent is all ready for the same condition."

"Well, all right. But it's not the usual thing. The hell with it. Look at that great big city. I wonder where my baby is in that mess."

"Your baby is prob'ly doing something romantic like riding home in a great big streetcar."

We dropped the line on top of the others.

The Chief came out on deck.

"There's that ugly city of St. Paul agin," he said.

Diamond arrived with a ratchet and threw it down. He leaned against the capstan and looked up at the city.

"St. Paul," he said. "Here we are, by god."

Or as Joe used to say: "The best thing about the city is it's so far from the country."

Sargent, invincible, cool, and fairly miserable, blew a long melodious blast on the whistle to open the Great Western Bridge. The echo reverberated off the post office slanting up into the sky beside us, and swept back to the airport across the river.

"You know what you sound like to me?" Joe said. "You sound like you didn't get no invite to the dance."

"All right, boss," I said. "Maybe you got the idea. And after all, I really like those pathetic boobs. You never know what kind of comic misinformation you'll hear from them."

"Someday even you will know what you're talking

about," Joe said, and I decided I was willing to wait for that wonderful day.

In the meantime the girls waved down at us as we passed under the Robert Street Bridge and our thoughts turned landward. Evidently the betrayal of the people by their leaders, the function of the individualist in a dynamic society, and the problem of *Man* v. *Golf Club* would remain neglected and unsolved by us for another twenty-four hours. The chimneys of the powerhouse, our destination, were already visible up by the Smith Avenue Bridge. Soon each of us could wander off into the big city to seek his own redemption and release, facing at last the inevitable hour of action or atonement.

dont talk to me
said the ringmaster flea
about human beings
what the hell are they
except something to eat

— ARCHY

23

THUS we entered St. Paul, on an evening in August, 1943. The Red Army troops were breaking German resistance near Kharkov, the U.S. Navy shelled the Italian mainland for the first time, and the Athletics lost their thirteenth consecutive game, to the St. Louis Browns. That's what the pilothouse radio said.

"Here's your coffee, Cap," I said. We were under the Smith Avenue Bridge, right below the power company coal dock.

"More coal. More coal for St. Paul," Sargent said. "Bill, you think we'll ever get it all moved up here? You think we'll ever get all that Illinois coal transplanted to Minnesota?"

"We just got to keep at it, Cap," I said. "We'll get it all moved."

"That's a damn tiresome story the way you tell it, Bill."

I went back down to the deck.

It was the end of the line. The coal dock was in a nasty little cut on the east bank, surrounded by box elder trees full of red bugs. We tied the tow off to the bank and busted the boat loose and went up into the cut and commenced yanking MTs out and tying them off below the bridge. Then we broke up the loads and shoved them into the hole and spotted them for unloading.

Then we ran the boat into the trees and got a line out and we were there.

"Where the hell are we, Pittsburgh?" the Junior Engineer said, coming out on deck wiping his face with a rag.

"That's right. Let's go up and have some of that Tube City beer," Joe said.

Sargent came down the forward steps.

"We'll wait on four empties," he said. "Then we'll go back down to Alton, Illinois, and get some more coal, just for the novelty of it."

We cleaned up the deck and left Diamond to hold her

down, and I went back and took a shower and shined my shoes and put on my gabardine suit. And a pale blue shirt and a foulard tie. And slicked my hair and got my money and went down the plank and through the trees to the road. I walked down the road past the powerhouse toward the city, and behind me some dark clouds rolled up over Cherokee Heights across the river.

I walked through the slums and the sun went down and it grew hotter. From open windows came the whining and snarling of man, that noble creature, and the sound of busting teacups, girdles splitting, slaps, shrieks, and mumbling. Through the shredded curtains plaster Kewpie dolls peeped above the iron bedsteads. In a side yard a bulldog lay dying. Screen doors slammed. The porches were falling off. Kids threw rocks at each other and a girl of ten offered me an invitation.

Down by the Robert Street Bridge the aging shuttle steamer *Demopolis* blew for the draw — a lovely mellow note from the Warrior River that spread out over the drab rooftops of the flats and floated up the bluff, even to the Hotel Lowry. These steamboat whistles will follow you everywhere: they come through the cracks in the window frames when you are making love, out on the farm you can hear them coming up the draws and through the barbed wire, you can hear them in your dreams, you'll hear them all the time. If you are getting tired of your girl because she is speechless and squeeze her little white throat, in a $2.00 room, until she is dead, and they send you up to Stillwater, the steamboats will come creeping up the St. Croix and blow those mournful whistles right through

[231]

the bars. You know that's no train whistle, don't you, boy? Makes you sad, don't it?

I climbed up the steep street out of the valley, past the morgue, where a little man sat in a chair on the sidewalk reading a book called *Honey Lou, or The Love Wrecker.* At the top I stopped and looked back over the flats. In the direction of North Dakota the sky was beginning to look terrible.

Where was Merle? Washing her gloves? Lying on the bed reading the paper? Reading one of my letters?

Through the dusk I could see the grain elevators, and the power plant chimneys, and a smear of neon showed where the tavern was. Some of the boys were there, downing twenty-cent shots with beer chasers, looking at the girls on the calendars, and running riot among the glassine bags of Korn Kurls. Some of them would get stalled right there, only a hundred yards from the boat, and never would get uptown, and after the joint closed they would sit in the gravel on the road, with paper bags full of bottled beer, and drink and tell of how wonderful they were and all the places they'd been, until the river began to stand on end and the box elder trees revolved slowly, around and around.

On the boulevard behind me the cars were swishing smoothly, to the accompaniment of gentle radio music and girlish laughter. Across the street were the tall buildings.

Merle and I were now in the same city.

I stood there looking down from the Acropolis at the plain below and the *Demopolis*, now up beyond the power plant, blew her whistle for the Omaha Railroad Bridge and

I felt sad about all the boys in the army — sweating, home-sick, getting their heads blown off.

Yes there was a war on all this time, at least so the radio said. The war went on, and it was hell getting a seat in a day coach, but when would I get promoted to Mate? Was Merle out with some mutt or putting flowers in her hair against my arrival? These are the questions that mean something. In seeking an answer to them we make novenas, consult the Koran, and ask advice from our inferiors.

I went in the first bar I met and threw one down. It hit bottom as I reached the phone booth.

She lived in a place with the phone in the hall and an unromantic voice answered and told me she wasn't home.

"Are you sure?" I said.

"Who is this? Rex?"

"No it ain't Rex," I said.

"Well, she ain't here anyway."

DROP 5 CENTS AND LISTEN FOR DIAL TONE

Only about an hour in town and now here's Rex on the scene. How could she love me and even know anybody named Rex?

I went back to the bar and pretended Rex was the manager of the movie house where she worked, calling her on business.

"Rex!" I said. "For god's sake what a love affair."

"What did you say, buddy?" the bartender said.

"Gimme a shot," I said.

"Any preference?" he said. He must have learned that at the bartenders' academy.

"Green River is OK." The whiskey without regrets.

[233]

God in heaven, where could she be? I wrote her from Winona and from Guttenberg when I'd be here.

"What for a wash?"

Outside the street lit up with a silent flash of lightning.

"Well, it'll be good for the crops," said a genius down the bar hanging onto a beer.

"Water," I said.

Then it thundered and the glasses in the back bar rattled and I wanted to see Joe. Everything had gone to pieces.

"We need rain bad," the bartender said.

Maybe she was down at the drugstore getting some bobby pins for her beautiful black hair.

"Been dry around here?" I said, looking at myself in the mirror and wishing I had a nose like Joe's.

"Terrible dry," he said.

Sometimes it seems as though half my life has been spent in bars talking about the prospect of rain, snow, or an earthquake. The wanderer's home away from home, a sanctuary for the lonesome sailor.

"Same here," I said, and shoved my glass across.

I gave up another nickel to the Northwestern Bell Telephone System.

"I'm sorry, mister, but she just ain't here, that's all."

I wasn't getting any further enjoyment out of looking at myself, so I went and sat at the end of the bar this time. Two soldiers were arguing about fish.

A very fine specimen of healthy Minnesota type girl came in and went on display exactly three stools away; any other time this would have been a grand treat but not now.

"Have you got a beer for a poor lost dirl?" she says in a baby voice which at once proclaimed her the cutup in her crowd. On top of everything else I had to sit here and listen to this stuff.

"Hello, Marge," the bartender said, and drew one.

Then she gave a fresh bulletin on weather conditions and I succumbed to the inevitable and announced that we had had plenty of rain and hail and avalanches and everything down below.

"Down below what?" says Margie.

"Down south," I said.

"Hastings, Red Wing?"

"Oh my god no," I said. "St. Louis, Rock Island, Dubuque."

"What do you do in all them places?" she said.

"I'm a government inspector in the Fish Department."

"I never heard of that," she said.

"Oh, it's a big thing," I said.

"Well, I learn something every day," she said and made away with her second glass of Schmidt's beer.

"That's the way it goes," I said.

"It takes all kinds to make the world," she said.

"Give Marge another beer," I said to the bartender as I went back to telephone.

"That there fella is in the government Fish Department," the bartender said to the soldiers.

This time I drew a juvenile delinquent who said Merle ain't there and she hadn't saw her all evening. All right then, somewhere in this great big amalgam of neon and concrete my little one was wandering around, or on a

streetcar, or in church — she could be anyplace including
the shooting gallery.

"If she comes in tell her Bill called and to stay right
there. I'll keep on ringing this thing until she is there."

"If you're so anxious for a date I'll meet you in twenty
minutes," the kid said.

"I don't want no date. Anyway you sound too young to
me, kiddo."

"I ain't either too young. You'd be surprised I bet. Are
you a soldier?"

"I'm Sergeant Flagg. Well — how old are you?"

"I'm thirteen but you'd take me for sixteen any day.
I know the ropes. Where'll I meetcha?"

"I was wrong. You're too old. I prefer a younger type
woman."

"You bastard!"

"You look like you lost your last friend," Marge said
when I got back.

"That's far from funny," I said. "Let's you and me move
on. I don't like the orchestra here."

There was no novelty to the events of the next two hours.
We went to a bar and another bar and another, and they
were all alike except for the brand on the beer spigots and
there was even a similarity there. That was the year when
you put a nickel in the juke box and it automatically played
"Pistol Packin Mama" until you busted a chair over it.
Every so often I would call Merle's house again and have
a ridiculous conversation with somebody. Marge and I
sat in a sticky booth and drank sticky drinks, and she
curled her fingers around my wrist, kissed my cheek,

smoked, laughed, and wriggled. She asked me where I got that tie and who was my favorite heroine of the silver screen. Had I been to Denver and why didn't I get a haircut? And she dragged me out into the rain from bar to bar, and my suit was wet with rain, and my mouth full of strawberry lipstick.

Then I thought I had to see Joe and that maybe he would be at the tavern down by the coal docks. So we got into a cab and bounced from curb to curb down the brick paving to the river.

"I don't like it down here," Marge said.

"Get out, god damn it," I said. "I've been in all your favorite dumps. This is where I live. Get out."

Mama Poznanski was tending bar and she said Joe had gone uptown about ten o'clock.

Vincent, the wiper off the boat, had a load on.

"You deckhands put on airs, don'tcha?" he said. "Well, ya don't look like so much to me just because ya got a necktie on."

This immediately led to a fight which ended very quickly when Vincent socked me on the chin and I lit on the dirty floor among the cigarette butts. That wiry little dog from Illinois gave me a dandy.

"All right," I said, "that's about enough of that for now."

Marge was crying and Mama Poznanski called us a cab and I took the girl home, through ten thousand empty streets, past grocery stores with the night light burning, past a billion telephone poles that staggered before me, and the girl cuddled me, strangled me with kisses, and invited me to stay with her.

"My roommate is real pretty. We'll have a swell time," she said.

I said good-by.

So at last I gave the driver Merle's address. Then there were more streets, stop lights, and frame houses with wet sidewalks in front under the trees, and then we were at Merle's place. The driver took my three dollars and drove off in the rain.

I went between the houses and looked up at her window. No light. Windows open. I went to the front again and sat down on the steps and the rain felt cool, and I said "Darling, darling, darling" over and over, and the leaves in the trees said "Darling" too, with the rain in them. It was late, and the big city around me was just making a few sounds — a train from Duluth blowing a yard whistle, a window tossed up, a car door closing, and more rain.

I had been there about half an hour when a cab pulled up and a guy came out of the house.

He went down the steps to the cab, and then came back. "Give you a lift anyplace, Mac?" he said.

"No," I said. "I'm gonna stay here for three days."

After a while I went and stood between the houses. "So this is the way the people live then," I thought, "in these houses, with windows that slide up and down." I went over and felt the six-inch drop siding on Merle's house. "That's good for keeping the rain out," I thought, and I looked up to the sky to see if I could see God looking down out of a rain cloud at his boy, and Merle's light was on.

I was about done.

I made it halfway up the stairs and sat down. I decided

I would crawl the rest of the way and save shoe leather. I got to the top, and like the drunk in *A Fool There Was*, I crawled across the hall, reached up and turned the knob.

There she was, all bare and beautiful, sitting on the edge of the bed and looking at me.

"My god what happened to you?" she said, and she kept on sitting there all bare and beautiful.

"It was love, my sweet, that laid me low," I said.

I woke up about five in the morning and the curtains were waving in a fresh breeze that filled the room with the damp smell of the city after the rain. My love was asleep. I pulled back the sheet and looked at her for a long time before I kissed her and felt her arms close around my neck.

Now it was seven o'clock.

"Well lover, now maybe you can tell me where you got hit by the truck last night," Merle said.

"These are awfully cute," I said.

"Aren't they though? But what about it? I never saw you in such a shape."

"Baby, who's this Rex?"

"What's *he* got to do with it?"

She squirmed away from me and out of bed.

"What's the matter with you?" she said, and she went over and stood by the window, looking at me. If there's anything more satisfying than a slender naked girl nineteen years old standing in the morning sunshine after a night of love I haven't found it yet.

"Tell me something, Venus," I said, sitting up and looking at her, "can you bake?"

[239]

"Bake? What do you mean 'bake'?"

"Can you bake a pie, or some biscuits?"

"I can't stand you when you get comical. You think you're damn cute, don't you? You better get up and get out of here," and she reached for her slip.

"Don't put that on," I said. "I'm not trying to be funny. Come here, little Miss Pinky-bit."

She came over and I pulled her down beside me.

"Listen kid," I said, "I love *you*. Who do you love, me or Rex or Irene or who?"

"I don't want to talk about love with a stuck-up, mean, nasty son of a bitch like you," she said.

"You're a sweet, fragile little rosebud, aren't you?"

"What you expect me to do, with you off on the dirty steamboat all the time? Sure I go out with Rex. I already told you that."

"I think you're awful beautiful," I said. "Let's have a drink."

"Oh, you're so crazy," she said.

"What a beautiful baby," I said.

"Don't do that, lover," she said. "Let's really have a drink."

"All right. Let's really have one."

So we did.

The next afternoon we were still tied up at the coal docks.

I came out of the messroom and stood looking at the river. Vincent came out of the engine room wiping his hands on some waste.

"That was a good one you gave me last night," I said.

"We was both drunk," he said.

"Don't use such rough language," I said.

He went back into the engine room.

Joe came down the deck.

"Say, you look pretty tough," he said.

"That's how I feel," I said.

"How'd you like my job, kid?"

"What's the joke?"

"Al goes back to the *Illinois* to go pilot. I move up to First Mate — and you move up to Second Mate. How's that?"

"That's a life sentence on the river," I said. "I guess I'll take it."

"How about the other thing? Did you make up your mind yet?"

"Yes," I said. "I made up my mind."

A dead carp floated past, bound for St. Louis.

Well, I should never have left home in the first place and I wouldn't be sitting here in the pilothouse thinking of Merle and the kids, just like Captain James Sargent used to do.

Bananas comes up to the pilothouse. He is a deckhand from Fountain City.

"Here's the mail, Cap," he says.

"Think you'll ever amount to anything, Bananas?" I say.

"I doubt it, Cap," he says.

"You got a girl, Bananas?"

"Well, I think so, Cap."

"Listen kid," I say, blowing the whistle at the East Dubuque drawbridge, "get off the boat if you've got a girl. Get a job in a filling station. Get a job sweeping out the Eagles' Hall on Mondays. Get a job greasing the drawbridge or picking gum off theater seats. But get off the river, Bananas, get off the river."

"OK, Cap," he says, not interested. Why — this damn deckhand is humoring me.

"Well, go on back down and get in the poker game," I say.

"We ain't got no game going," he says.

"Go on. Beat it," I say.

I've got another letter of Merle's in my hand. Now she has taken to writing me on pink paper.

AFTERWORD

RICHARD Pike Bissell was born in Dubuque, Iowa, in 1913, the son of Frederick Ezekiel Bissell and Edith Mary Pike Bissell. His father owned a clothing factory, and the family lived in a big house at the top of the Fourth Street inclined railway. As a boy he heard the deep-throated steam whistles and smelled the steam-cylinder oil that floated from the engine rooms of the excursion boats that stopped in his home town. In those days commercial traffic on the Mississippi was at a minimum. The river was constantly being dredged to keep open a six-foot channel, and the ineffective wing dams that still plague river pilots were being built. But

Bissell was to see great changes in his life on the river: the first diesel engine appeared on the inland rivers in 1931, and before much longer the working days of the steamboat were over.[1]

At fourteen he built a rowboat in his basement. At sixteen he took Mark Twain seriously enough to run away with a friend to raft "like in the book" downstream from Winona. Their adventure did not work out exactly as they had imagined, but it was nonetheless wonderful and "dreamy" in its own way.

Bissell graduated from Phillips Exeter Academy in 1932 and from Harvard College in 1936. Thus, as he later wrote, he was to become the "only second cook on the entire Mississippi-Missouri-Ohio river system who qualified as a licensed anthropologist." After a brief interlude as a salesman for the Polaroid Corporation, he shipped as an ordinary seaman on the American Export Line to the Mediterranean. Then, with the river still in his blood, he returned to Dubuque and became a deckhand on the big, old sternwheeler, the *James W. Good* of the Federal Barge Line. On February 5, 1938, he married Marian Van Patten Grilk of New England and left the river to begin domestic life on a salary of $28.50 a week in the family business. Much to the consternation of his parents, this life was lived with pride and joy and

[1]Autobiographical information and quotations are from Richard Bissell, *My Life on the Mississippi, or Why I Am Not Mark Twain* (New York: Little, Brown and Co., 1973) and *Who Was Who in America*, vol. 7 (Chicago: Marquis Who's Who, Inc., 1981), 53. The author would also like to thank Marian Bissell, Richard's widow, for her help.

a real four-poster bed on the *Prairie Bell,* the "finest houseboat on the upper Mississippi."

But it was a different river from that he had known as a boy. It was being transformed from the free-flowing Mississippi into a canal whose nine-foot channel was stabilized by the engineered stairway of the twenty-six locks we know today. By 1939 the great pathway was opened to the diesel-powered tows that would move tens of thousands of tons of coal up the Mississippi to St. Paul during World War II.

The war "busted up" the Bissells' idyll on the house-boat as it "busted up" everything. Turned down by the navy for poor eyesight and not fancying the army, Bissell enlisted to work in earnest on the river. In 1942 the towboat that "became home" on the Illinois and "beautiful upper Mississippi" rivers was the Central Barge Line's 1350 horse-power diesel, the *W. A. Shepard.* When Bissell looked back on his career he would see himself once more "on top of the pilot house of the *W. A. Shepard.* . . . I am polishing the searchlight . . . in the middle of the wide sunny valley, moving slowly up the river with our hopes and our youth, and our coal." In the midst of these pleasures, he grew the distinctively professorial mustache he was to keep the rest of his life and decided to go for his mate's and then his pilot's license. "Don't laugh," he wrote to his wife. In the novel *High Water,* the struggling, overburdened *Royal Prince* passes the old *Shepard,* reconditioned and renamed the *Wheelock Whitney.* It is interesting to know that in 1961 the *Wheelock Whitney,* renamed the *John Paul,* was to sink, with her engine room flooded, above the dreaded Keokuck lock.

In the winter of 1942–43, Bissell spent three months on the Ohio aboard the big steamer, the *Alexander Mackenzie.* This experience, he wrote, was what really "cut the souse" with those who examined him for the license of "Mate of Inland Steam Vessels," a title that "had been conceived, tested, and frozen solid in the days of the packet boat." On the *Mackenzie* he had been officially third mate and second cook, but the Master Pilot's recommendation is more accurate: "He has substituted for the watchman or second mate and his work has been very satisfactory at all times. And also I think that any one who can do the work satisfactorily on a boat as large as the steamer *Mackenzie* and with tows as large as she handles is capable of holding a mate's license." Though Bissell found things pretty glum aboard this fancy steamer, there were "plenty of exciting times and one big grounding," and during a flood the boat nearly ran out of fuel.

With this "Rosetta Stone of my life" in his suitcase, Bissell went back to the *Mackenzie* as deckhand, but he was soon transferred as mate to the *Minnesota,* an "old style, coal burning, hand fired, high pressure sternwheel steamboat." She was a "curiosity" even in wartime when every boat and every pilot was pressed into service. Built as a pleasure boat by Dr. William J. Mayo of Rochester, Minnesota, she had tile bathrooms and dozens of electric fans and was definitely not meant for heavy work. The trip on the Tennessee River, towing grain and pig iron, was "lousy" and "slow" and often dangerous. Still, like most pilots of his generation, Bissell preferred the smell of "escaping steam and soft coal gas" to the diesel engine rooms where no moving parts were visible and which "don't smell right."

Bissell received his pilot's license in 1943, having successfully drawn from memory a map of the upper Mississippi on the scale of one inch to the mile. Today on the river, sonar depth finders with digital readouts supply much detailed information on the river channels, and a pilot's skill is more severely tested in negotiating long, heavy tows around bends and through locks than in knowing the river channels. Bissell would deplore the monotony aboard tows that can no longer afford any landings. And air-conditioned pilot's lounges, clean living quarters, and fresh milk would draw his scorn. But the six-hour shifts that even he found strenuous are still the rule, and Jane Curry, in her first-hand account of tows today, tells us that technology has not cured the independence and pride of rivermen. The modern river, like Bissell's, is still "a school of natural and human variety."[2]

In 1943 this river school was to put the new pilot's sardonic but good-humored wit to a severe test. Rather

[2]Jane Curry, *The River's in My Blood: Riverboat Pilots Tell Their Stories* (Lincoln: University of Nebraska Press, 1983), 262. A pilot's hand-drawn test map is reproduced on page 44.

than piloting the upper Mississippi, he found himself "sold" for one hundred dollars a month "to slavery on the coal barges of the Illinois river and the Chicago Drainage Canal." Again he worked aboard the *Wheelock Whitney*. In 1944, he was on the Monongahela River as pilot of a "dirty old boat with a telescoping pilothouse and a single stack." From this grubby but exhilarating experience came his first published article, "The Coal Queen," which later led to the book, *The Monongahela*, one of the most informative, amusing, and certainly the most personal of the Rivers of America Series, published by Rinehart from the 1940s to the 1960s.[3]

But Bissell is more than a reporter. He is an artist whose style creates a world distinctively his own. With this book and its companion, two of his river novels — *A Stretch on the River* (1950) and *High Water* (1954) — have been brought back to print. His first novel, *A Stretch on the River*, is largely autobiographical in content, but it is also a well-constructed story with a skillfully maintained mood of excitement and suspense. In spite of a shared background, Bissell is not his protagonist, Bill Joyce. If he is anybody aboard the *Inland Coal*, he is everybody. Even in his day, Bissell chronicled a vanishing America, but the river remained unchanged, with

[3]Bissell, "The Coal Queen," *Atlantic Monthly*, June 28, 1949, and *The Monongahela* (New York: Rinehart, 1952). Bissell's other river books include *Goodbye Ava* (New York: Little, Brown and Co., 1960), set on a houseboat in Dubuque, and *How Many Miles to Galena* (New York: Little, Brown and Co., 1965), which has several chapters dealing with river towns.

[248]

"the smell of mud and burdock leaves, nettles, wild grapevines, bugs and sink holes" and "islands and willows and railroad ties and mud . . . like Minnesota and Illinois and Wisconsin and Iowa and part of Missouri, all mixed up together."[4] It is all uniquely Bissell—the river towns with their moldy bars and lovely names that constantly roll off his pen, the decaying urban waterfronts (how he would have ridiculed the aluminum arch in St. Louis!), and the girls, the mysterious, beautiful girls.

All of these joys reflect the boisterous and fervent love of life and youth that characterized wartime, working USA. In A *Stretch on the River*, sex is a rowdy, picaresque theme accentuated by the thoughts of the deckhand, Joyce. The book was not recommended for public libraries by the *Library Journal*. One reviewer remarked that while Mark Twain would have liked it, his "genteel wife, Livy" would not.[5] In *High Water*, the "girl problem" strikes a muted note (see p. 86–87), but Bissell's rollicking humor does not hide the true horrors of racism as the boat passes Kincaid County, Illinois, where things were as they were "back in the days of Tom and Huck" (p. 57).

And Bissell is indeed funny. As Bernard DeVoto, his most thoughtful and perceptive critic, wrote in a review of A *Stretch on the River*, he has "a genuinely comic per-

[4]Bissell, A *Stretch on the River* (New York: Little, Brown and Co., 1950; St. Paul: Minnesota Historical Society Press, Borealis Book, 1987), 200, and *High Water* (New York: Little, Brown and Co., 1954; St. Paul: Minnesota Historical Society Press, Borealis Book, 1987), 129.
[5]*Library Journal* 75 (July 1950): 1176; *Time* 56 (July 24, 1950): 84.

ception, which is exceedingly rare."[6] His style, with its random, non-sequitur dialogue and his comic use of detail, can be compared to that of another "original"— Charles Dickens, who might have created Curly, Iron Hat, Diamond, and the luckless Shorty, with his "random mixed socks." True humor is not, however, without pathos. The drowned Shorty's monologue gives inexpressible dignity to this unessential life.

Inevitably, Bissell was called a "modern Mark Twain"—a tag to which he definitely objected, explaining with semi-serious criticism of the master why he, Richard Bissell of Dubuque, Iowa, was not the reincarnation of someone else. In the end he summed it up: "Everybody's life on the river is different. Sam had his and I had mine." In *High Water*, he joked about the problem; in Hannibal, Missouri, the mate of the *Royal Prince* is haunted, as Bissell had been since boyhood, by a "crummy-looking," white-haired old man with a drooping mustache dressed in a "dirty old white linen suit" (p. 149). Characteristically dubious of literary pretension, Bissell would have preferred to be compared as a pilot to George Byron Merrick, author of *Old Times on the Upper Mississippi*, whose book he much admired.[7] For if Mark Twain's untamed river has flowed through American intellectual and social criticism in countless

[6]*New York Herald Tribune Book Review*, July 23, 1950, p. 7.
[7]Merrick, *Old Times on the Upper Mississippi: The Recollections of a Steamboat Pilot from 1854 to 1863* (New York: Arthur C. Clark Co., 1909; St. Paul: Minnesota Historical Society Press, Borealis Book, 1987).

lectures, books, and college courses, Bissell's river defies such treatment. It is a love affair with engines, beautiful black coal, steel barges, and work—about which he is always serious.

The same year that *High Water* was published, the Broadway musical "The Pajama Game," based on Bissell's 1953 novel *7½ Cents,* was a smash hit. This coincidence is significant in light of the original typed manuscript of the novel.[8] It reveals that Bissell had sent his publisher a classic tragedy, beginning with the brooding grayness of St. Louis and building up through the doubts of the crew as to the abilities of the pilots of the *Royal Prince,* to the disappearance of One Eye from the tied-off barges. And the eternal rain.

But by 1954, in the mind of his publishers, the novelist Bissell was subordinated to the talented producer of entertainment. Though Bissell's humor flashes through the darkness, the tragedy of *High Water* was apparently thought to be too great a departure from his reputation as a humorist. He was persuaded by his editor to introduce the young woman stranded on the roof of a farmhouse (p. 174). The insertions from then change the whole tenor of the work and can now be seen as intrusions.[9] The last three chapters, which were added in the revision, can be contrasted to the end of *A Stretch on*

---

[8]This manuscript is in the Richard P. Bissell papers, Special Collections Department, University of Iowa Libraries, Iowa City.

[9]See particularly published p. 218-24 and manuscript p. 171-72. Here a philosophical mood is broken by the scene in the woman's cabin.

the River, where the deckhand stays with his "life sentence" on the river thinking of the kids and home just "like Captain James Sargent used to do." But does the love story truly relieve us of the tragedy which, in Bissell's original version, ends abruptly on page 241, leaving only the hero, the nameless messboy, the comic Arkansaw, and the heartless Jakoniski left alive? Would the public have accepted such a stark ending?

Richard Bissell moved back to Dubuque, Iowa, in 1975 from Rowayton, Connecticut, where he had been living for a number of years. He died in Dubuque on May 4, 1977; his wife and four children survived him.

—*Martha C. Bray*

9 780873 512202